REBAR

Christopher Gardner

PAGE PUBLISHING
Conneaut Lake, PA

First originally published by Page Publishing 2023

ISBN 979-8-88960-449-5 (pbk)
ISBN 979-8-88960-456-3 (digital)

Printed in the United States of America

Introduction

Have you ever wondered where you would find yourself if you dug a hole from where you are now on planet Earth to the other side of the planet in a straight line? Most of us have. Probably as a child, you were pondering this along with all the other questions children often ask their parents, questions such as "Why is the sky blue?" or "Why can't we see air?" or, the big one, "Where would I come out if I tunneled through the Earth?"

Relatively speaking, it could be done, but scientifically speaking, it could not. Why? One answer is that the center of the Earth is 10,800 degrees. Other reasons can be found by researching what scientists have found through their studies and written about. I'm not going to list all of them, but if you are interested in the makings of the center of the Earth, the information is already available. Most people nowadays would be like "I'm good" anyway.

In this story, I'm going to be using antipodes and what they are and how they work. An antipode is a way of finding a way from one spot on Earth to the opposite side in a straight line. An antipode is defined as the true opposite. To figure out where you would be on the other side of Earth in relation to where you are now, longitude and latitude lines would work, if you know the formula to use. I'm not going to spoil the fun by giving the formula to you. If you're interested, it can be found.

You could take an old globe and straightedge to find your opposite, but that is not going to be exact.

If you do become interested and want to know where you would come out on the opposite side of Earth, and you find the longitude and latitude formula, not to burst anyone's bubble about coming out in some exotic location, more times than not, you will just come out at the bottom of an ocean, being that the Earth is seventy percent water. But there are places that you will tunnel out to land. I'm going to use a couple of actual places in this story.

Between me and you, the reader, it would be wonderful to be able to travel through the center of the Earth. The old saying that we all learned in school is, "The shortest distance from two points is a straight line."

Here is a fun fact: it would take forty-two minutes and eight seconds to go from one side of the Earth to the other side if you were to go straight through a hole that was already dug. Of course, you would be free-falling at a high rate of speed because of the Earth's tilt and rotation speed. Let's see thrill-seekers line up for that ride.

There are many facts and studies on digging or drilling through the center of the Earth. There are studies and even games on antipodes. The story following this intro is my take on antipodes and tunneling through Earth. I hope you enjoy this adventure.

Chapter 1

Ding. The elevator announces its arrival on the third floor. It is Monday morning at the School of Geography, which is in a three-story brick building tucked in between residential houses that have been turned into a law office on one side and an accountant's office on the other side. The avenue in front runs east and west, and facing north is a large university. April McKenzie is standing in the elevator, waiting for the doors to open.

"Open. Come on, open," April anxiously exclaims, wondering if today is the day she is going to be stuck on this old out-of-date elevator. "Please, please open!"

The doors finally open. They are wobbly, with a clattering noise of a roller with a flat spot on it.

"Oh, thank heavens," she says, stepping off the elevator quickly, in case the elevator changes its mind and traps her for meanness.

"Good morning, April," Tina Gordon says. Tina is a coworker and good friend of April. She walked out of the office they both work in when she heard April in the elevator asking the doors to open. She thought April might be trapped.

The office at the School of Geography employs three full-time employees: Tina, April, and Steven. The three are graduates of the School of Geography. Enrollees at this school are mostly students from the university across the avenue that need an extracurricular credit. But for April, Tina, and Steven, they chose the School of Geography to major in geography and mapping and to make that field their careers. After graduating, and not wanting to move away, they each applied for employment with the school, each one coming to work at different times. Tina Gordon has the most seniority, having graduated and started working ten years ago; then Steven

1

Smith with eight years employed; and finally, April, who, at the age of fifty-two, graduated and with some help from Tina was hired a year ago.

"Elevator scares you, again?" Tina asks April. "I heard you talking to it."

"I wasn't sure if the doors were going to open. That thing gets slower and noisier every day. I certainly didn't want to start this week waiting on the repairman to get me out," April replies, looking back at the elevator.

"It is an old rickety piece," adds Tina, smiling at April. "Did you have a good weekend? Go out with anybody?" Tina asks with a wink at April.

"Weekend was good. Just stayed home. How about you? Did you and Ricky do anything?" April asks.

"Not much. We grilled out Saturday evening. That's about it. I would have invited you over, but I figured you were out on town with some hot piece of meat," answers Tina, holding the door to the office open.

"Oh no, no. I just stayed in." April blushes.

Tina picks up a memo note from her desk. "I have this for you. Professor Henderson wants to see you."

April looks at the note and asks, "Did he say what about?"

"Nope. He handed it to me and kept on walking."

"I guess I'll go see him. I'll be right back," April says, setting her purse and lunch bag down on her desk chair.

Professor Tom Henderson's office is at the end of the hall on the right side (the same side of the hall as the elevator) across from the classroom. The School of Geography professor is fifty-two years old and six-foot tall, with long gray hair, kind of salt and pepper, which he keeps in a ponytail. He has been teaching geography and mapping classes for twenty-five years. He was married once to his college sweetheart for five years but has stayed single since their divorce. He figured that since he was going to be accused of having affairs with his female students, which is what his wife had been accusing him of doing, he would be better off staying single. That way he could definitely entertain his female students hassle-free.

Professor Henderson has always adored April McKenzie. She is just the right type of girl he likes. Not too tall or too short, she is five four and blonde, but not yellow blonde, more dirty blonde. He absolutely adores her, especially how she looks with glasses.

Since April stopped seeing Chris, whom she dated for five years, Professor Henderson has enjoyed every chance he gets to see her. The two have gone out a few times, secretly, not wanting anyone at the School of Geography to know, because the rule is "you cannot date students or colleagues." Of course, Professor Henderson knows how to get around that little rule. It is simple. Do not tell anyone.

"Knock, knock," April says, standing in the open doorway to Professor Henderson's office.

"Hey, April, please come in. Have a seat. Would you like some coffee? Just made it," a smiling Professor Henderson says standing up. He is wanting to act professional toward April and not show any emotional attachment. Rumors have been circulating for years that there are cameras throughout the school building, inside and outside, and someone somewhere is watching the goings-on at the school.

After April sits in the chair in front of his desk, Professor Henderson moves around the desk and leans against the front.

"How are you? I haven't seen you in a long minute." Leaning into her right ear trying to make it look like he is picking lint off the shoulder of her blouse, he whispers, "Sorry, I haven't called you in a few days," smiling at her as he pulls away.

"You wanted to see me?" she asks, leaning to her left, away from him in case he tries for a kiss while he is this close.

"Yes," Professor Henderson says, standing up straight, turning, and returning to his desk chair. Sitting across from her, he starts, "Yes, April, I have an assignment that I think you would enjoy. You have been here a year, I believe, and as you know, we get assignments from time to time. You haven't been on one yet, and this assignment would be right for you. It came to my attention Friday. It could be a big one. I got a call from my bosses at The National Geography Board. They are needing someone to go to a construction site to look at something."

"A construction site. Why would they want to send a geographer to a construction site?" April asks, amused.

Professor Henderson leans back in his chair. "Let me see if I can explain this to you. A construction crew was digging ground for a new building. They were digging down for the subfloors, when they hit a rock. At least they think it is a rock."

"A rock!" April exclaims, leaning forward in her chair.

"Yes," replies Professor Henderson. "A rock, but this is where the story gets weird. The construction crew hit the rock with the bucket on the backhoe. The rock did not break. It didn't even scratch it. I was told they tried breaking the rock with the bucket. They tried digging it up. All they accomplished was breaking the bucket on the backhoe into pieces."

Professor Henderson looks across his desk at April, through her U-shaped glasses, green eyes behind them.

April looks at Professor Henderson, brow wrinkled. "Why would you want me to go look at a rock? I'm a geographer and a mapper. What does this have to do with that?" she asks, wondering.

Professor Henderson put his hands on his desk and says, "Okay. Here is what I do know for certain. There have been all kinds of people from archeologists to paleontologists who have been looking at this rock. None of them have seen anything like it. They have hit it with hammers, no scratches, no chipping, no nothing. They have dug down beside it. They finally brought in a drill. They drilled four hundred feet down beside it, but it continues on downward. There seems to be no end to this rock."

Professor Henderson continues, "When I talked to The National Geography Board on Friday, I said something to them that, I guess, gave them another direction to go with on this. I told them that maybe this thing goes all the way through Earth to the other side. They said that that could be possible, amazing, but possible."

April falls back into her chair. She looks around the office. She looks out the window at the outside world. Finally, she looks toward Professor Henderson. She says, "Tom—" She uses his first name. He has asked her to call him Professor Henderson at work after their first date to play it safe. She did what she was asked, even as their romance started turning more serious.

"April," Professor Henderson cuts her off. "I know. Why does the government want a geographer and mapper to look at a rock? The answer is this. You did a study on antipodes for your dissertation paper."

"I did. You gave me a C on it." April sits straight in her chair. "You told The National Geography Board I did a paper on antipodes?"

"Yes, I did."

"That's why you want me to go look at this rock. You and they think it is an antipode and that it runs through the center of the Earth and out the other side." April smiles.

"It's a theory, April. I told them about your paper on antipodes and the calculations you did in your findings. They want to explore this angle. Nobody that has been to the construction site knows what it is. They don't even know what kind of rock it is. All I know from talking with the Board is they want to pursue this theory and maybe, if this is an antipode, find out where the other side is located. I know it's just a theory. Heck, you or anyone could say it's a conspiracy theory, but they want to look at all possibilities. Anyway, you haven't done an assignment yet. I think you can do this one."

"Are you going to be doing this with me?" April asks, looking Tom in the eyes.

"I wish I could. But I have classes to teach."

"We're a college. Professors are allowed to do research."

He looks across his desk at her, wishing he could go with her but also knowing what the college would say about colleagues going out in the field together, thinking they would want to do more than work together. This college and its old school, out-of-date, values. They really need to get with the times of today. A male and female can work together. But enrollment is good. The graduation rate is outstanding, for a small college. He is not going to ruffle feathers. Professor Henderson laughs and says, "You'll have to find someone else. The National Geography Board said they would pay for one person's expenses. That would be yours."

"Can I take Tina?" April asks.

Professor Henderson shakes his head from side to side.

"I've got to have her here since Steven is out with his and Jill's new baby and the complications they're having with her."

"Spina bifida. That poor baby girl. Steven and Jill too," April says, feeling remorseful for Steven and Jill. Their first child. She was supposed to be happy and healthy coming into this world. But three months after being born, *bam*!

April knows Steven and Jill could handle the diagnosis of spina bifida, them two being the most patient, kindest couple. She remembers Steven coming to work beaming with joy about his first child being born and then the diagnosis. Steven was crushed, she could tell, but he stayed positive. He is always positive.

April, not having any children of her own, was just as crushed upon hearing the diagnosis of the baby.

April looks Tom in the eyes and says, "I've got to have help." Then she asks, "Where am I going, anyway? Where is this rock thing?"

"Hong Kong," Tom answers. "It's in Hong Kong. Your flight is already booked, and a hotel room is reserved for you. You leave tomorrow."

"Oh, wow. That soon," April replies. "I still need to have help. If it is what they think it might be, I have to have someone on the other side of the world to see if it is the other end."

Tom puts his hands up. "Don't you have any friends that could help you?"

April shoots back. "You know I don't know many people. And those people I do know would not do this for free. You know my story."

Professor Tom Henderson winks at her. "I know. Well, I can think of one person we both know who might help. And he would probably love to do it, for you, especially," Tom says with a little smile in the corner of his mouth.

April looks at Tom and stutters, "C-C-Chris."

"Yes."

She rolls her eyes. "Oh, wow. I haven't spoken to him in nine months. When we parted company was the last time I talked to him."

"Call him. He would probably love to hear from you."

"I don't know."

"Call him. You know he loves adventure. This would be right up his alley, an adventure and being with you."

April sits back in her chair looking perplexed at Tom and asks, "Do you still talk to him?"

"I haven't in a while."

Still looking perplexed, she asks, "Would you call him? It has been so long for me, and I did say some mean things to him. I called him immature."

"Tell you what." Tom chuckles. "Go to Hong Kong, do some research, and if you think this theory might have some merit, call him, ask him to help. Like you said, you need someone on the other side of the world. You wouldn't have to see him. You two would just be talking on the phone."

"And you would be okay with this?" April asks, play-slapping Tom's hand.

"We're not exclusive. Are we? You said you wanted to go slow. Plus, Chris is a pretty good guy. A little wild. Look, he likes to have fun. Everything's an adventure," he says. "You two have a history. I would be okay with you two talking on the phone, working together. Half a world apart."

What Tom does not understand and April surely is not going to tell him is that she still has feelings for Chris. April and Chris parted ways after April was hired full time by the college. April thought Chris acted immature when they were around other people with the college. He was always trying to make a joke about anything. He would not dress appropriately for functions she was supposed to attend. He always wore blue jeans, but he would wear a nice button-up shirt.

April was always embarrassed to tell people Chris was a truck driver. Even though he owned his own business, truck, and trailer and made great money doing it, it still embarrassed her.

Other people seemed more mature to her, or their spouses were something that came with an impressive title. She just could not make herself see that Chris was happy with his job and happy for her and her accomplishments.

Chris always told her he loved her, even in front of other people, and she knew he did. She loved him dearly. When she had made full-time status at the college, she changed.

After they parted ways, Chris would still call April, but she would never answer the phone. When he stopped calling, she then realized she missed him; she still cared deeply about him. They did have a history, a good history full of laughs and adventures.

Now, she is worried that if she did call him and ask for his help, what would he say to her? Would he be mean to her like she was to him?

She has gone out with Tom Henderson, secretly, for dinner or drinks, nothing beyond that realm, definitely nothing sexual. Even at fifty-two and considered by some to still be a good-looking woman, she knows she is not too old for sex. The thing is, Chris was the last man she had sex with, and she wants him, Chris, to be the next guy she sleeps with, not Tom, Mr. professor of geography and mapping, a long-haired womanizer that she knows he is.

She sits in Professor Tom Henderson's office, looking at Tom, him saying he would be okay with everything if she talked to Chris on the phone, him on one side of the world and her on the other side, April smiles and to herself thinks, *I will call Chris, maybe to apologize, maybe not, at least just to hear his voice and find out what he has been up to these past nine months. Hopefully, he is not seeing anyone. That would probably hurt.*

Yeah, she will call him for help, but first she has to get ready to go to Hong Kong, a world away from where she is now.

"Well, all right. I'll go to Hong Kong, do some research, and see what I can find out."

Tom looks at her, thinking how her eyes are so mesmerizing, so clear and bright, wishing she would speed things up between them, so he can see if her body is as beautiful without clothes on as it is with the outfits she wears to work and the teasing outfits she wears on their dates. He asks. "Are you going to call Chris? See if he'll help you?"

"Let me get to Hong Kong and see if I am going to need him." She winced a little at her last two words. Of course, she needed Chris. Talking about him has stirred a new desire in her. Finding the nerve to call him is going to be the tough part. Maybe he has forgiven her.

As she starts to leave Professor Henderson's office, Professor Henderson asks her, "What do you say we go out for drinks, later?"

Stopping at the door to his office, she turns and says, "I have to get ready," and she walks out into the hall.

Chapter 2

The life of a truck driver is different from other people's lives. Truck driving is a passion; it gets in your blood. Many people do not understand until they too become one.

The open road is where a truck driver sits in their little corner office of an eighty thousand-pound machine, watching the scenery and landscapes change by the minute, different places, different faces everywhere. Some of the faces are friendly, and some of the faces are not so friendly. People say, "All you do is ride around." Au contraire, there is a lot more to it than just riding around.

The life of a truck driver. We are here, and we are gone, just like that. It is the perfect life for a serial killer. Make your delivery here, and be two or three states away in a matter of a couple of hours. Time is a truck driver's worst enemy. Appointment times—that is the time the customer has set for the truck driver to arrive at their location. If you show up early for an appointment, the customer will ask you to wait somewhere until it is your time to be there. If you show up late for an appointment, the customer will tell you to reschedule for another time slot and leave their property until then. If you show up on time, you are at the mercy of the customer. The life of a truck driver is best described by the quote: "Hurry up, and wait."

The weather that a truck driver has to navigate through. We have seen all that mother nature can dish out.

The four wheelers—family cars and pickup trucks to the common people are everywhere, cutting in and out, zipping past without a care in the world. It is amazing to watch from the seat of a big truck those people with their "I gotta be first at all cost" attitudes challenging big trucks. It makes one wonder if people are trying to commit suicide by big truck.

The accidents, the big truck versus the four-wheeler, vice versa—these accidents are almost always going to be the truck driver's fault. They are the professional drivers, held to a zero tolerance for accidents. That is the number one reason why dash cameras are so popular with truck drivers, but still, even with video evidence, four-wheelers still want the "big check."

Chris Collier has been driving a big truck for ten years, north, south, east, and west. He does long hauls and short hauls. If the load has dollars to be made and he wins the bidding war for the load, he will run it. He is not only a truck driver, but he is also a business owner. Owning his own truck and trailer and a business name has been a dream come true for Chris.

In a previous life, before Chris got into trucking, he did construction work. After living in hotels for fifteen years, losing his high school sweetheart he was married to for ten years, and almost being permanently disabled, he started looking at other avenues of work to try.

Truck driving is the path Chris decided to go with. The opportunities in trucking were what he was looking to achieve. Although not a glamorous occupation, trucking offered Chris a chance to be a business owner. Him not being married anymore; his children at the age where hanging out with dad was not cool anymore, as their friends were more important; and his health were all the deciding factors in his decision. He set out for training through a driving school, found a company to hire him, and set out on the road of learning.

Ten years into professional driving, owning all of his equipment, being debt-free, getting to pick and choose what he wants to haul and where he wants to go, and making great money, Chris does not dread waking up in the mornings. He is healthy, and his children are a big part of his life and excited for him. Although still not married but was really close to doing that not too long ago, Chris is definitely happy with his life right now.

Rolling home after a prosperous week out on the road, Chris stops daydreaming. He has been dreaming of his former girlfriend. *Water under the bridge,* he thinks to himself. Checking his mirrors again, he sees the sign for his exit, home time. He is excited, even though he has no plans for the weekend or the following week other than to rest and stay out of his truck.

Getting off at his exit from the interstate, Chris feels his left side vibrate. Not able to look at his phone screen to see who is calling, he pulls down the microphone arm of his phone headset and pushes the button to answer.

"Hello."

"Hello, Chris?" asks a familiar female voice.

"April?" Chris asks, recognizing her voice, her soft, easygoing voice, a voice he would recognize anywhere, a voice he has longed to hear.

"April McKenzie? Or is it Dr. April McKenzie now?" Chris asks.

"It's April. Just April McKenzie. No doctor," April replies smiling and feeling very nervous and full of anxiety about making this call.

"How are you, girl?" Chris asks excitedly. He does not believe he is hearing her voice, a voice of the girl who broke his heart months ago. The one girl or lady—she is definitely a lady—Chris has yearned for these many months since they had parted.

Immature. She called me immature and said she did not want to be with me anymore. How that word, *immature*, had scarred me. The aches and pains my heart suffered because of that word. I thought things were going great with us, April and me together, me on the road, while she was going to school. We were spending time together on weekends and talking on the phone during the week. We were two people in absolute love with each other.

Then, she got the job, a job at the college she had graduated from in geography and mapping. April was so excited when she was notified she had been hired as a full-time employee, no more interning.

After all the excitement had died down, April started looking at me differently. I am easygoing, maybe too easygoing; fun; and sometimes funny. She started comparing me to her work colleagues and their spouses and friends. April thought they looked down on me. She thought they made fun of me and my profession. So she broke it off with me, only to find out afterward that I and one Professor

Tom Henderson, the head of the School of Geography, her boss, had become friends, as well as some other people from the college. But it was too late. She had called me immature and an embarrassment to her and her new friends, her work friends.

"I'm good," April answers and then asks, "How are you?"

"I'm good. Doing good. In another hour, I'll be home and doing real good," Chris answers, shocked to be hearing from the lady he loved, still loves.

He had called her after the breakup, but she would not answer her phone. After calling for nearly two weeks, he gave up. Chris had hoped this day would happen, and here she is, on the phone.

"You're on your way home?" April asks, the anxiety building in her more as she prepares herself for this conversation. She hopes that he has forgiven her and will not bring up the past, their past. She, also, hopes she can bring herself to ask him for the help she is going to need.

"Yes, yes. On my way home. Another week of outrageousness behind me. So, April, what do I owe this phone call from out of the blue too?"

April takes a breath. *So far, he seems to be his usual self,* she thinks to herself.

"Well, I need some help."

"You called me out of the blue for some help. And what kind of help might you need my assistance with, may I ask?" Chris asks, smiling. He is hoping this might be the makeup call he has been longing to receive.

"I am on an assignment with work. I have been doing a lot of research, and what it is that I am working on has the potential to be very big," April says, following the script she memorized for this call. She made the script to ease her nerves.

"How big?" asks Chris.

"Earth shatteringly big. Totally mind-blowing. Chris, I really need help with this. I'm not lying. This is going to be huge, that is, if I'm right with the information I have."

"And you called me?" Chris is being facetious.

"Chris, yes." April took a deep breath after answering. So here it comes. Here is the moment I have dreaded. He is going to let me have it and so soon into our phone call.

April contemplates hanging up. She thinks to herself, *This is a mistake. This is my mistake. I should not have called him.* She asks Chris, "Can you hang on for a minute?"

"Sure," answers Chris.

April puts the phone down on her bed. She puts her head in her hands. The script is not working. She is trying to convince herself to keep talking to Chris. She takes another deep breath. She looks over at her phone laying on the bed. She whispers to her hands, "I need help. I do not have many friends outside of work. Chris is my only option. I need him. I really need him."

April stares at the floor. Whispering to herself, again she says, "Okay, April, calm yourself down. If he is going to let me have it for what I said about him, so be it. Let's get it over with. You need him. Hopefully he has moved on and forgiven me. Wait a minute. Did I just say moved on? Stop it, April. Keep your emotions in check. Hopefully, he has forgiven me. Let's leave it there."

April picks up her phone. "Chris, are you still there?"

"I'm still here," he answers.

"Okay, good." April breathes in through her nose. "Chris, yes, I called you. You are the only person I could think of to ask for help. I don't have anyone else who can help me. So please hear me out."

"I'm listening," says Chris.

April is feeling her anxiety bubbling up through her chest. She continues, "With the research I have done and with your help that I really need, I should be able to prove what I think will change everything—the way we look at Earth, this planet that we are standing on right now. This is going to turn absolutely everything we know about this planet upside down. This will completely trash all the information we have been given from scientists, schools, and anyone who has done research about planet Earth and how it is held together."

"That big, huh?" Chris remarks. "I thought you were a geographer and a mapper? Now, you're looking at what's holding the Earth together, and I'm the only person on said Earth who can help you?"

"I am and you are," April replies.

"Nobody else at that college can help you?" Chris asks.

"Nobody, Chris. They are all busy."

"And you don't know anyone else?"

"No, Chris. Listen. You are the only person I trust to be able to do this with me. I know you are very capable of doing what I need you to do. Will you help me?"

"Hang on. First off, before I say yay or nay, tell me what you have found and what you think is going to blow minds, everywhere."

Smiling and starting to relax, April begins to explain, "Do you remember the paper I did in college, for my dissertation? The one on antipodes?"

"Antipodes?" Chris asks, not remembering.

"Yeah, antipodes," April answers. "I explained them to you. You know, if you were to tunnel through Earth to the other side in a straight line, where would you come out?"

"I vaguely remember you telling me something about those." Chris lies. "That was a long time ago. I mean, geeze, I've slept since then, that was so long ago. April, really, what are you needing me to do? Tunnel through Earth, come on, you can do that yourself."

April chuckles and says, "Oh no, I'm not tunneling through anything. I don't need to. But I do need you, if you will, to go to a place that is opposite from where I am."

"And do what?" Chris asks.

"Find the other side of this rock."

"A rock? Uh, April, really. What do you mean a rock? Where are you, anyway?" Chris almost had to pull his truck over to the shoulder of the road because he was so dumbfounded by what April had said to him.

"Chris, just hear me out. I can explain. I have been studying a rock that has been found. The rock is not a typical rock. A construction company was digging down into the ground for a building that is to be built when they hit this rock. They tried to dig it up, but it would not budge. They dug down and around the rock to try blowing it up with explosives. That did not work. The blast didn't leave any kind of mark or scratch on the rock. They brought in a drilling machine and drilled beside the rock a good four hundred feet. They lowered cameras down to see if they could see the end of the rock. This rock literally continued on with no end in sight that anyone has been able to find." April continues. "My theory, and the theory of the people who sent me on this expedition, is that the rock goes all the way through the center of the Earth, straight through to the other side. The college sent me here because of my studies and the research paper I did on antipodes. If I can prove this theory, this will be a major discovery of epic proportions."

Chris adjusts in his seat and stares out the windshield. At the moment, he is speechless, thinking in another thirty minutes, he will be home.

He speaks into his headset, "So let me make sure I understand what you are telling me, April. You want me to help you find something that you and your people have a theory about, no facts. Just an idea, a wild dream, basically."

"Yes. I know it sounds crazy, but with your help, we can prove this theory."

"These antipodes. You said they run in a straight line, right?"

"Yes, yes, they do. An antipode is a true opposite."

"Okay, April. Why don't you just do this? Go to the opposite of where you are, and see if this rock is sticking out there."

April replies, "I thought about that, but I need someone over there to help me make sure it is the same rock."

"Okay, take a picture of the rock there, and then go to the other side and see if it matches. Wouldn't that work?"

Getting frustrated now, April answers, "No, Chris, It wouldn't work."

"Yeah, you're probably right. So your people sent you on this expedition because you did a paper?"

"Yes, they did." April replies. "Listen, I know this is hard to believe that this could be possible, but I want to see where this theory goes, where this rock goes. I need to know. I have come too far to stop now. I really need to know, and I need your help."

"Are we talking for a day or two or what?" Chris asks.

"If the theory proves to be true and this rock does go through to the other side of Earth, I'll need you for a week, maybe longer."

"A week or more, huh?" Chris asks. "Well, that brings me to my next questions. Who is paying for this? How am I going to be paid?"

"Are you going to help me?" April asks, excitedly.

"You gotta answer my questions first," replies Chris.

"Okay, Chris." April is dreading what she is about to tell him. "You will have to pay for your own travels and provisions. The National Geography Board would only pay for me, and I don't have enough money to pay you or your expenses." She begins to cry. "Please, Chris, I need your help. Do it for me."

"Wow, I mean…wow, April. You don't think I'm still, what was the word, oh…immature? You don't think I'm too immature? I mean, that is what you told me the last time we talked."

Crying and having her anxiety crush her and thinking of the mistake she made calling him immature, April begins to plead. "Please, Chris. You are the only person I know who can do what I need done. I trust you. We have always worked well together on everything we have done." Still crying, she continues, "I made a mistake. I am sorry for calling you that. I am sorry for everything I did. I really need your help. If you will help me, I will figure out some way to repay you. If this theory turns out to be true, this discovery will change history, at least what we know about Earth."

Chris heard the passion and sincerity in her voice. She said she was sorry and she needed him. Driving down the road, going home, he feels his heart pounding in his chest. His eyes are watery. This is the call he had been wanting for the past few months. He has been wanting to hear her voice again, the voice of an angel, his angel, April McKenzie, the woman he still loves.

"Chris, are you still there?" April asks, softly.

"Yeah, I'm still here," he answers, just as soft.

"Will you help me, please?"

Heart still pounding and eyes still wailing up, Chris wipes them with his sleeve. He thinks, *The past is the past. We can't change it. She is here now, on the phone. She needs help. She is asking me for it.* He says, "Yes, I'll help you."

April screams with joy. "Thank you!"

Chris says, "I'll make some calls when I get home, to let my brokers know I'm going to take a little time off. What do you need me to do?" He is smiling, now. A sense of calm has come to him. He has an opportunity to do something with April. His prayers have been answered.

April says, "I need you to go to La Quiaca, Argentina. When you get there, I'll have the information you will need to go to where I think the other side of this rock is located."

"Holy cow, girl. Is this where we are going to meet?"

"No, we won't be meeting. You'll be there by yourself. I'll be here on the opposite side. Make sure you bring a phone charger and your passport."

"The opposite side? Where are you?" Chris asks.

"I'm in Hong Kong," April replies, laughing.

"Hong Kong!" he exclaims.

"Yes." April giggles. "Hong Kong is the direct opposite of La Quiaca. If you were to draw a straight line through Earth, we will be pretty close to opposite of each other."

"This is sounding crazier by the minute."

"It's not too crazy. Listen, I'll send you the coordinates to the rock when you get there. You should be able to find the rock with your GPS."

"When do you need me in La Quiaca? Did I pronounce that right?" Chris asks.

"Close enough. Work on your Spanish on the way. And I need you there as soon as possible."

"Well, okay. I'll get going as soon as I can. I can already see my phone bill going through the roof." Chris jokes.

Laughing, April says, "Chris, thank you so much for helping me with this. I promise, I will repay you for everything."

"Hey, it sounds like an adventure of a lifetime."

"That's why I called you," April says, overcome with happiness. "I know you love an adventure."

"That is so true. You know me best."

"Call me when you get to La Quiaca, Chris. We'll get this project started."

"I hope you are right about this, April."

"I hope so too. I'll talk to you soon, and thank you, Chris."

"You're welcome. I am definitely looking forward to talking to you again," Chris says, excitedly.

"Bye, Chris. Please be careful," April replies, smiling.

"Bye, April."

Chapter 3

The flight from Birmingham to Buenos Aires is no small task. After more than fourteen hours of airtime, Chris is glad to be on the ground. He has an hour of wait time before the small plane he had to rent for the trip to La Quiaca is ready. He had thought about driving to La Quiaca, but after some research he did, he decided the rent for the small plane would be more beneficial than the twenty-hour drive across an unfamiliar country. The drive would have been interesting, for him, but he drives enough every day.

Chris loves the different sceneries. That is the best part of his job. Crossing the country, seeing all that there is to see, the beauty of the scenery across the United States is an attribute for him that gives meaning to life.

Looking over maps of Argentina on his flight down made him wonder what beauty this country beholds. The drive from Buenos Aires to La Quiaca is probably a beautiful experience, especially for someone who has never been here, but April did say she needed him there as soon as possible. Some other time, he will make this trip.

The plane he rented has been fueled, and the pilot has explained the safety protocol to him. For the next six hours, they will be in the air. Chris has asked for forgiveness from the Almighty above, fastened his seatbelt, and placed a firm grip on the "Oh crap" handle.

Landing on the only dirt runway at the Aeropuerto La Quiaca, which is located a few miles outside of La Quiaca, a town situated on the northernmost border of Argentina, Chris begins to have serious concerns about what he has agreed to do for April. He knows she needs help, but looking out the window of the single engine plane he had to rent, plus he had to tip the pilot a hundred dollars because the pilot said that that was the rules, he sees one lone building at the opposite end of the dirty runway. Through the dust they had kicked up on landing, he is trying to decide if the building is not abandoned. Thoughts begin to enter his mind as the pilot turns the plane toward the building that the pilot said is the terminal. The first thought he has is "Are you serious?" and then came "What the hell am I doing?"

He tries to shake the thoughts from his head. He says to himself, "This is for April. You agreed to do this. Now, smile and be happy. You're here."

In the back of his mind, trying to get past the "This is for April" part, the little devil on the left shoulder keeps saying, "You have got to be kidding me." He continues to stare, with a dumbfounded look on his face, at what he is seeing.

As the plane pulls alongside the terminal building, Chris's negativity rears up, again. Holding back more cussing, he notices there is no car rental office. He sees a sign on the door to the terminal. It says, "Cerrado." Remembering his Spanish words he learned on the flight to Buenos Aires, Chris knows it means "closed."

Stepping off the plane, Chris takes his bag from the pilot, who is telling him in broken English that the airport is closed for the day. It is late in the afternoon. He tells Chris he has a friend with a truck who can come pick them up and take them to town, if he needs a ride. Chris nods yes. He figures that is his only option other than walking. He hopes there is a hotel in town that is open.

Chris has brought plenty of money with him, not really knowing much of what he is going to be getting into on this trip. He is holding out hope that April will be able to repay him for his expenditures. He is already down about six thousand dollars. The flight to Buenos Aires and the plane to get here and also the pilot who is very friendly, but a very scary pilot, have costs.

Sitting on a bench in front of the airport's only building and waiting for the pilot's friend with a truck to appear, Chris calls April.

She answers on the second ring.

"Hello, April. I hope you can hear me. I have very few signal bars."

"Hey, Chris. Yes, I can hear you. Are you there?"

"I'm somewhere. The pilot said I am outside La Quiaca a few miles. I'm here with him waiting on his friend with a truck to pick us up and take me to a hotel he said is in town. Very nice hotel, he tells me. So how's Hong Kong? I'm guessing there are people there, unlike here."

"Oh, Chris, I'm sorry. Maybe when you get to town, there will be people around. Other than no one around, was your trip good?"

"I'd have rather gone to Hong Kong. Buenos Aires was nice, from what I could see of it."

"Well, I need you there, and thankfully you made it," April adds.

"Yes, I'm here. By the way, what time is it in Hong Kong?"

"It is four in the morning. Monday," she answers.

"I'm guessing I woke you up. I'm sorry. I should have checked the time difference. It's five in the afternoon, Sunday, here," Chris says sympathetically.

"Oh, it's no problem. I wanted you to call me when you arrived. When you get checked into the hotel, are you going to rest, or do you want to see if you can find the rock?"

"I'm going to have to get some sleep, April. It has been a long journey, and talking to the pilot about this place, he said La Quiaca pretty much rolls up the sidewalks at dark, and he also said not to be outside after dark."

"Okay, that'll be good. That will give me a chance to get the information I will be sending you absolutely correct. So it is eleven hours' difference between Hong Kong to La Quiaca. Let's say I will call you at five this afternoon, my time. That will make it six in the morning there, and we will find the other side of this rock."

"That sounds good. At least we will be on the same day. April, are you going to be able to gain access to the site after hours?" Chris wonders.

"I should. I'll tell them I'm about to find the other end of this rock, plus, they know me here," April answers.

"Well, all righty, until we talk again, which will be tomorrow for me. Bye, April."

"Bye, Chris," she says and pushes the end call icon on her phone screen.

April tosses the bed covers off her and puts her feet on the carpet of her hotel suite. After stretching and yawning, she begins to feel the excitement building in her. She is finally, after being in Hong Kong for nearly two weeks, going to see if the theory that she has convinced herself is true, really is. She is going to see if this rock is a rebar holding the Earth together.

April turns on the coffee pot and heads for the bathroom. Excited that Chris has made it to La Quiaca, Argentina, which is supposed to be the direct opposite of Hong Kong according to her research on antipodes, she turns on the water for a shower. Stepping into the warm water, April starts going over her research and all the discoveries about the mysterious rock in her head. Hoping she has everything in order, April steps out of the shower, dries herself, puts on her robe, and calls Tom Henderson.

"Hello, April," Tom Henderson answers.

"Hello, Tom," April says back. She is calling him with an update. "Chris is in Argentina at that little town."

"You have talked to him? How did he sound? He wasn't mad at you, was he?" Tom Henderson asks.

April replies, "No. He sounded fine. Tired."

"Good. At least he is there. Did you give him his directions to that church where the rock should be?"

"No, not yet. He wanted to get some rest before we got started. He was waiting on a ride into town when he called me. But he's there."

"So are you excited, nervous? This is the moment we have been waiting for."

"Both. I want this to be true."

"Me too. Was Chris's spirit upbeat, or did you maybe sense from his tone of voice that he thought he might be getting used?" Tom Henderson asks.

"I'm not using him, Tom!" April replies angrily. "He sounded tired, and from the trip he just made, I can say I would be worn out too. He's gonna help me, Tom. He is the only person that would."

"I would have done this with you, April, but you know why I wasn't able to."

After taking a sip of her coffee, April smiles and says, "So you're just going to be uncomfortable with my ex-boyfriend helping me, huh? Are you jealous? I did not think you were that type of person."

"April, I'm not jealous, by no means. I think Chris still has feelings for you, and I don't want to see you get hurt."

"First of all, Tom, I don't think Chris would ever hurt me, and anyway, I thought you two were supposed to be friends?"

"Well, I haven't really talked much with him since you two parted ways. When I did, it was usually about you."

"Tom, he said he would help me. That is what he is doing."

"April, darling, I'm okay with Chris helping you. Yes, he can help you. I'm just looking out for you. He still has feelings for you. All I want is for you to be careful. Maybe I am a little jealous, I don't know. Anyway, if this goes according to the plan, you will only be talking to him on the phone, not seeing him."

April sighs loudly. She did not want to have this conversation with Tom. She was wanting to give him an update. That is all. She knows she has feelings for Chris, and she hopes he still has strong feelings for her. This is none of Tom's business. His business is about the rock. To get away from this topic, she adamantly tells Tom, "Listen, if he still has feelings for me, so be it. I'm thinking he has moved on. He is over it. Over me. I hurt him pretty badly, Tom. But I needed help with this. He said he would help. He's in Argentina now. So let's just focus on this rock, and when I call him to give him his information, he will continue to help me, and he will stay friendly to me, the way he has been every time we talk. Okay?"

"Okay, April. What time are you supposed to talk to him?" Tom Henderson asks, happy to change the subject.

"At six in the morning, his time," April says, still annoyed.

"What time will that be in Hong Kong?"

"Five in the afternoon," April replies, calming down.

"So that would make it seven in the morning, Birmingham time. Am I correct?" Tom Henderson jokingly asks.

"You're supposed to be the smart one, Professor, but yes, that is correct," April answers, smiling at his joke.

"Will you call me after you talk to Chris?"

"I will, Tom."

"Thanks, April. Talk to you later. Bye."

"Bye." April throws her phone on the bed. She takes a sip of her coffee and stares out the window.

Not seeing Chris is going to be hard. Maybe after this is over, we can get together. See what happens. I apologized to him. He has been friendly. Tom and I are not going anywhere. Actually, Tom is the immature one, not Chris. What a big mistake I have made. Chris and I have a good history. Hopefully, we can make more.

It has been a while since I have seen Chris. I can just imagine the look on his face when he saw my name on his caller screen. I hope his face lit up, and a smile came across his face from ear to ear. Reflecting back, April is glad she made the call to Chris. She is happy that he answered. That made her giggle. He sounded like the same guy I fell in love with. Now, he is on the other side of the world.

Tom has no reason to be jealous. He does not want to be serious with anyone, and I do not want to be serious with him. All he wants to do is chase the young students who do not know any better around and have me turn the other way while he does this. Chris never did that. He is a real man. Why did I not stop myself and see this? I called Chris the immature one. He is not. I am.

Chapter 4

Chris hears his phone chirp. It is the chirp telling him he has a text message. He reaches over to the nightstand and picks up his phone. It is a text from April. He reads it, and reads it, again. The text is written partly in English and in Spanish. He makes out that the text is directions to a series of Spanish words he is unfamiliar with seeing. The end of the text says she will call him shortly. He looks at the time on the nightstand clock, almost time for her to call.

Chris has been staring at the ceiling of his hotel room, still feeling the effects of his trip. He does not want to move, even though he has to use the bathroom. The bed is just too comfortable, and he is suffering from what he figures is jet lag.

He thinks April must be anxious to get started, sending him text messages. He stretches, hearing his body protest this maneuver with popping from all over his body. He settles back down on the bed and stares at the ceiling some more.

He reminisces about yesterday leaving the airport in the pilot's friend's truck. When they were about two miles from the airport, the right rear tire came off the truck. He learned after they retrieved the tire and mounted it back on the truck, the tire did not have any lug nuts to hold it on. The pilot's friend said that someone stole the lug nuts off of all the tires, probably out of meanness. He said two tires came off on his way to the airport. I asked what he was using to hold them on, and he said he tied some wire to the tires and studs.

No more tires fell off after that; they drove very slow to town, making it to a restaurant that was starting to close for the day. Getting food for dinner, they took a very slow trip to the only hotel in town. Seeing the hotel from the outside certainly did not make him comfortable, but once he was checked in and got into his room, he saw how nice this place really is. The inside, he rated it a five star.

Transfixed on a certain spot on the ceiling, it takes Chris a moment before he realizes his phone is ringing. He reaches over to grab his phone from the nightstand, and he sees April's name on the screen, when the phone is snatched from his hand. He still had it plugged up to the phone charger that he forgot about. Fumbling with it for a few seconds, he is able to unplug the cord and answer on the tenth ring.

"Hello," Chris says with a frog in his throat. He clears his throat and says it again. "Hello."

"Hello." Came April's voice through the speaker. "Did I wake you? I was beginning to think you weren't going to answer." She had the feeling that he had left or was just ignoring her. She was panicking.

"I'm awake," Chris says. "I forgot I had my phone plugged up, charging. I almost dropped it." He reached down to unplug the cord from the wall socket.

Chuckling under her breath and feeling relieved, she asks, "Did you see the text I sent you?"

"Yeah, I saw it. What were all those Spanish words?"

"Spanish words?" April asks, not remembering the text.

"Yeah, some of the text I could read. The Spanish words I wasn't familiar with."

"Oh," April replies, looking back at the text. "The Spanish words are the name of the cathedral you are going to."

"That's a long name for a church. Is the building as big as the name?"

"It's a cathedral, not a church," April corrects Chris.

"My apologies. You think the rock is going to be in this cathedral?"

"That's what the longitude and latitude coordinates are showing. They show it being at the Iglesia Nuestra Señora del Perpetuo Socorro cathedral. I looked it up. It is a very old cathedral," April explains.

"And these directions will get me there?"

"Yes. Do you have a ride to get there or do I need to find you one?"

"You can do that?"

"I can, if you need me to."

"No. I have a way. The hotel lady at the desk said I can borrow one of their bicycles to get around. The friend with a truck, the pilot's friend. Funny story. The wheels on his truck tend to fall off when we were moving. So he's not available."

Smiling, April says, "I'm sure that was interesting."

"I'll tell you about it some other time."

"I'm sure you will," April says, laughing. "And I'm trying to visualize you riding a bicycle."

"Hey, you know what they say, it's like riding a bike."

"Very funny, Chris." April laughed. "Let's go over the directions. Are you near highway nine?"

"It's the main road through town. It's a block over from this hotel."

"Okay, so from what I've pulled up, take highway nine north to San Martin, and go east till you reach Ave del los Estudiantes. This should lead to a park, town square type of setup. The cathedral is in the northwest corner of the park."

"All right. I'll get going. Are you at your side of the rock now?"

"I will be. It's only a few blocks from me."

"Okay, April. I'll call you when I get there, or would you rather I call you when or if I find the rock?"

"Call me when you find the rock. And Chris, you will find the rock."

"I sure hope so, April. Talk to you, soon."

After ending the call with Chris, April calls Tom Henderson.

"Hey, darling. Has Chris found the rock?" Tom Henderson asks, answering his phone on the first ring.

April rolls her eyes at the "darling" remark. "He's on his way to the cathedral now," she answers.

"Good," says Tom, sitting at his desk with his feet up on the desk. He is looking over some notes he had written on a notepad. "I had a call, last night, from The National Geography Board. They were checking on our progress. I told them our progress is starting to pick up. We have everybody where they are needed."

"Why are they all of a sudden showing concern?" a bemused April asks.

"They had some information and wanted to see what was going on. I'm guessing that if this antipode theory is correct, they will want to be the ones receiving all the pats on the back and all the other accolades. But anyway, you have talked to Chris, and he is on his way to the cathedral. That's good. Maybe he can find the rock, and you two can verify it as the same rock."

"What information did the Board have, or am I not supposed to ask?"

"Yeah, that. They said they think they have another rock."

"Another rock. What? Where? Are you serious?" April asks excitedly about the news.

"Yes. Another one has been found in Honolulu," Tom answers. "Some guys were digging a trench in the ground to run electrical lines when they hit it. They tried to dig it up, but like your rock, it wouldn't budge. They called in a group of rockhounds to look at it. They described it as having the same makeup as the one you have."

"It is the same kind of rock?" April asks, sitting up straight in her chair and wondering why these rocks are suddenly appearing out of nowhere.

"It is. It has a smooth black glass-like outer shell. They said when they looked to see what they hit, there wasn't a scratch on it, anywhere. That's what I was told. It did, however, destroy the trench digging machine," says Tom.

"Oh my goodness." April shouted. "Am I going to Honolulu after we finish with this rock?"

"Assuming the rock in Argentina matches your rock, yes, and sweetheart, I'm going to be joining you on this one in Hawaii."

April almost dropped her phone.

"Oh!" She exclaims.

"Yeah, April, I'm going to take some vacation time. Are you excited? I'll get to join you and try to be of some help."

"Yeah, Tom, that sounds great. Um, hey, Chris is calling me. He must have found the rock. I'll call you later, Tom. Bye."

April places her phone on the table beside her chair. She feels like screaming. She rests her elbows on her legs and puts her head in her hands. She begins to cry. She wishes Chris would call. He has to have made it to the cathedral by now. Crying into her hands, she shakes her head side to side. She is fuming at Tom and his jealousy of her talking to Chris. She picks up her phone and looks at her call log. She starts to tap Chris's name but hesitates. She lays her phone back down. She knows Chris will call when he finds the rock. She wipes her eyes.

The conversation with Tom floods her thoughts. He used two pet names for me. He has never called me anything other than April. And to make me very uncomfortable, he is going to meet me in Hawaii, if I get to go. What do I do?

She stares at the floor for what seems like an eternity.

Her phone rings. She looks over to it on the table. Chris's name is on the screen. She collects herself and answers.

"Did you find it?" April almost yells answering the phone.

"What happened to hello?" Chris deadpans. "That's usually how phone calls start."

"Sorry," April replies, cracking a smile. "I got excited. So did you find it? Please say you did."

"Not yet, the cathedral doesn't open till eight o'clock."

"So we wait another hour, huh?"

"Yes, ma'am, that's the only choice we have. I did, however, talk to someone. That's why I called you. She didn't deny that there was something here. She noticed me wandering around the cathedral. She asked what I was looking for, and since I don't look like the locals, she had me busted as a suspicious person acting suspicious. Anyway, we began talking, and she spoke very good English. She allowed me the opportunity to explain myself about what I was looking for. I told her about the rock that goes on forever in Hong Kong and that there are people with more education than me hoping the other end of it is here."

"Did she believe you?" April asks.

"Well, I believe she did. I'm not in jail, anyway. She did tell me I had a crazy good story. But she also added that she had heard stories about something mysterious being found here when this place was built so many moons ago."

"What did she say it was?"

"She said she was told by older people who were around that there is a black diamond under the cathedral that has mystical powers, but she didn't think it was a rock, like a normal rock that we see all the time."

"Is she an older lady, young?"

"She is an older lady. She did move around very well for her age. She even had one tooth left. She showed me. She said when this one goes, she would not be far behind."

April smiles, enjoying this light banter with Chris. "Did she say anything about what those mystical might be?"

"She told me a story that she said she was told by the old-timers when she was young. She said that people from all over the area would come to the cathedral. They would go down into the basement, where the black diamond was located. These people would place one hand on the black diamond, where they would experience a tingling sensation, kind of like an electrical shock. It was well known in town and around the area that the black diamond could heal ailments."

"That's it, Chris. That has to be the other end of my rock," April says enthusiastically.

"I don't know, April. Did you feel an electric shock or a tingle when you touched your rock?"

"I haven't touched it without gloves on. Chris, this has to be it. The description she gave looks like a black diamond. It's the same as my rock. They are in a straight line with each other as an antipode is described to be. What more proof do we need?" April asks, shaking with nervous excitement.

"For starters, we need to make sure the rock is still here. The lady said she thought they removed it a long time ago."

"It can't be moved, Chris. Many have tried here. All have failed. If it goes straight through Earth, there is no way to move it. It has to be still there."

"I understand, April. But we need to be sure. She told me another story about a man who went down to the basement and placed his hand on the rock. When he removed his hand, he couldn't move. He was frozen in place. Then, all of a sudden, he took off at a fast pace, not quite running but walking real fast. He walked right into the front wall of the basement. He stepped back and hit it again, harder. The people who were down there with him tried to turn him and pointed him in the other direction toward the stairs. He would just snap back around and crash into the front wall, harder each time he hit. The last time he hit, she said that he jumped up from the ground and ran to the stairs. She said after that, the clergy stopped allowing people in the basement. She said that sometime later, they had the black diamond removed. She said she didn't know where to, but that was the story she was told."

"Now, that is a weird story. I wonder what caused that to happen," April opines. "But it has to still be there. It can't be moved. And I have the other end of it, here."

"Look, all we can do is wait until the cathedral opens. I'll see if I can get access to the basement and see if I can find it. I'm on the same page as you are, April. Let me see what I can find out, and I'll call you. Does that work for you?"

"Yes, that will work, Chris. I think I can make myself wait a little longer. I'll keep my fingers crossed that this is to be."

"I'll keep mine crossed that they allow me access to the basement."

April presses the end call icon on her phone screen. She claps her hands together. Smiling from ear to ear, she grabs her bag of tools and leaves her room for the construction site.

April exits off the elevator and crosses the hotel lobby still smiling. She knows she is right. She can feel it. This is the moment she has been waiting for, the rock she has here has an end to it, and Chris has it on the other side of the Earth.

She is happy for another reason too. Chris and her just had a great conversation together, a mature conversation. She is in love.

Leaving the hotel and starting down the street to the construction site, it hits here. She has to pee. Knowing that Chris will be calling her soon and wanting to be ready when he does call to make this history-changing discovery, she decides to hold it. She tells herself she does not have time to go back to the hotel.

Refocusing her attention to her task, she walks on down the sidewalk, hoping Chris will be able to BS his way into the basement.

Chapter 5

Early in the morning in La Quiaca, Argentina, is no different than any other small town. Most of the population wakes up to start their day traveling to the nearest big city for work. In La Quiaca, the nearest big city is across the La Quiaca river from Villazon, Bolivia. The rest of the population stays put, taking care of small-town business.

At eight o'clock sharp is when Iglesia Nuestra Señora del Perpetuo Socorro opens for business. At this time, Chris Collier is standing at the front doors listening to the locks being unlocked. The doors swing open, and Chris is surprised to see a nun, with only the head covering part of her habit on. The rest of her attire is khaki pants and a white button-up blouse. She is holding the right-side door open and kicking down the doorstop with her foot. She looks at Chris and smiles.

She says to him in Spanish, "Good morning, senor."

Chris smiles and replies to her in very amateurish Spanish, "Good morning, Sister."

She can tell immediately this person does not speak Spanish fluently, and in perfect English, she asks, "May I help you with anything this morning?"

Taken a little off guard by her perfect, unaccented English, Chris answers, "I sure hope so. My name is Chris Collier. I am from the United States. I have come here on a research project."

Opening the other door and putting the stopper down, she turns back toward Chris and says, "I am Sister Abigail Cortez. Nice to meet you, Chris Collier. What kind of a research project would bring you to this place?"

"Well, ma'am, I mean Sister, what brings me here is I am looking for something. I have a partner who is very smart, and she said I would find it here at this cathedral," Chris replies being coy with her.

Sister Cortez gives Chris a suspicious look, sensing she knows what he is looking for. She asks, "May I ask what the something is that you and your partner think is here?" Sister Cortez stares directly into Chris's eyes. She admires his tact. She says to herself, *I know what you are looking for, and like everybody else who has come here for it, I will turn you away too.*

"Can I come in?" Chris asks her.

Sister Cortez looks out past Chris into the park across the street. There are a few people milling around over there. She looks back at Chris and smiles. She says, "Well, first, tell me what it is you think is here, and I will tell you if it is or not."

Chris is still playing coy with her, not wanting to just come out and say what it is he is here to see, but sensing that she knows what he is here for, he tries a different, more honest approach. Chris looks directly into Sister Cortez's eyes and says, "Sister Cortez," holding his hands up in front of him, "I'm not here seeking glory or looking to be healed for anything that ails me. If I could come in, I promise, I will tell you the truth of what it is that I have come here to find out."

Sister Cortez looks around the park again. Looking back at Chris, she says, "Mr. Collier, you said you have a partner. Where is your partner?"

"She's in Hong Kong, China."

Sister Abigail Cortez's eyes become enlarged after hearing his partner is so far away. Her mouth forms into an "O" shape. She stares at Chris, thinking this man is here for some other reason. He has to be. He has been beating around the bush with me. He knows I know what he wants to see. He knows it is still here, or does he? He has not tried to force his way to it like some have. Maybe I should hear his story.

She regains her composure. "You said she's in Hong Kong. And you're here."

Chris simply says, "Yes, Sister."

"Okay, Mr. Collier. You have garnered my interest. You may come inside," Sister Cortez says.

"Thank you, Sister Cortez," Chris says, offering his hand to her, which she takes, gently, and shakes.

"Come with me, this way, to the office."

Entering through the door marked office behind Sister Cortez, Chris takes a seat in the only chair that is in front of Sister Cortez's desk.

"Would you like a cup of coffee?" Sister Cortez asks, pouring herself a cup.

Um, no, thank you," Chris answers, leaning forward in the chair.

Sister Cortez sets her coffee cup down on the desk and sits in her chair. She looks across the desk at Chris and says, "I know you are here about the black diamond. So what's your story? What are you and your partner researching?"

"I am here about the black diamond, Sister Cortez. What my partner and I are researching is, we are wanting to find out if the rock here is the other end of the rock she has in Hong Kong."

Sister Cortez's eyes get really big. She takes a sip of her coffee and then asks, "She has a black diamond like this one here? Are you kidding me?"

"No, Sister Cortez, I'm not kidding," Chris says, and he begins telling her the series of events that has brought him to La Quiaca, Argentina. He tells her the theory they have that the two rocks are one and the same.

"Mr. Collier, this is fascinating. And an antipode? Explain that to me, please."

Chris uses his fingers to draw an imaginary picture on her desk as he explains, "Let's say you and I dug a tunnel straight through Earth to the other side from here, where would we come out? In this case, according to my partner, who did a research paper in college on antipodes and ran the longitude and latitude numbers to pinpoint the exact opposite of La Quiaca, we would come out in Hong Kong. La Quiaca is directly opposite of Hong Kong. These two places are farthest from each other than any other place. That is what an antipode is, a direct opposite."

"And you and your partner think the rock here is an antipode?" Sister Cortez asks, full of excitement.

"That's what we want to find out," Chris answers.

Sister Cortez opens a side drawer on her desk and pulls out a set of keys. "Follow me, Mr. Collier. I'll take you down to it."

"So it is still here?" Chris asks, standing up.

"You know it is," replies Sister Cortez.

Arriving at the bottom of a narrow staircase into the basement at the back wall of the cathedral, Sister Cortez turns back to Chris and asks, "Have you heard any of the stories about this mystical black diamond?"

"I have heard a couple," Chris answers. "I especially like the one about the man who crashed into the wall several times after he touched it."

"That's the incident that made the elders stop allowing people down here to touch it. That rattled a lot of nerves," Sister Cortez comments, warily.

Chris asks, "You're not going to get into any trouble for allowing me down here, will you?"

"No, no. Mr. Collier, there have been numerous people who have come here through the years wanting to see it and touch it. They all have some silly story they have come up with trying to get to it. I will tell the elders what you told me. Your story is the most legitimate one I have heard since I was appointed here. If you and your partner's theory is correct, they will be happy to know that the mystery of its origins will be solved. Now, as to its powers, what do you think that may be caused by?"

"That, I don't know," Chris answers.

They walk to near center of the basement. To the left of the main walkway is a square opening in the floor with a wooden ladder poking out that is attached to a handrail that goes around the opening. Sister Cortez stops and points down to the rock. Chris looks over the handrail and sees the shiny black outer shell of the rock. It sits about three feet below floor level with about two feet of the rock above ground level.

Sister Cortez begins telling Chris more history. "They found it when they dug out for this cathedral so many years ago. This is why we have to go upstairs to get into the cathedral. The original plans had the cathedral being built at ground level. They couldn't move the rock." Looking down at the rock, Sister Cortez adds, "It is pretty, isn't it?"

"May I climb down to it?" Chris asks, staring at the rock. He stops staring and checks his phone to make sure he has a signal down in the basement.

"Yes, by all means," Sister Cortez says with enthusiasm. "I wouldn't touch it without gloves on, Mr. Collier. It supposedly gives off an electrical shock, at least that is what I have been told."

Chris climbs down beside the rock. He puts his phone headset on his head and looks up at Sister Cortez. "Sister Cortez, thank you for allowing me down here. I have to call my partner, and we will see what we can find out."

"Oh yes, of course. I'm going to leave you with it. If you need anything, just shout, and Mr. Collier, please be careful."

"I will. And thank you, again, for allowing me this access. I'll let you know what we find out, if anything, when I'm finished."

As Sister Cortez walks back to the stairs, Chris pushes April's name on his phone screen.

"Guess where I am," Chris says when April answers the phone.

"What happened to hello?" April asks, playing. "I'm kidding. I hope you're at the rock."

"I am."

"Oh, good. Did you have any trouble getting to it?"

"No. Nothing I couldn't handle. I told the truth. Sister Cortez is very excited to know what we find out. Are you at your end of the rock?"

"Yes, I am," replies April, excited.

"Okay, so what's the plan? How are we gonna do this?" Chris asks.

April answers, "I was thinking that if you hit it with a hammer, really hard, I will put my stethoscope on this side and see if I can hear you hammering. I also have a meter I can attach to the rock that reads vibrations."

"Uh, April, dear. Please don't take this the wrong way, but you do know how big Earth is right? If I hit this thing with a hammer, it would take a month before you would get any kind of reading."

"Well, that is all I could think of to do," April says, her feelings hurt a little bit. "What would be your bright idea?"

"I don't know. Let's think about this for a minute. There has got to be something we can do," Chris says, scratching his head.

"Well, don't take too long. I have to pee," April says, still reeling from his earlier comment and feeling her bladder swelling. This was not supposed to take too long.

"Really, April." Chris chuckled, trying not to sound frustrated. "Tell you what. Go pee, and we'll see what we think of when you get back."

"There is nowhere to go here," she says, hearing the tone in his voice and getting agitated herself.

"It's a construction site, April. Surely, there is a porta-potty around."

"I don't like using those. You know that." April almost shouted at him.

Shaking his head, laughing at this situation, Chris calmly asks, "Well, can you hold it until we figure this out?"

"I'll try," April replies, hearing him laughing. "Stop laughing at me."

"Okay. I'm sorry, but it is funny."

They are both silent for a moment. Each lost in thought about how they could be able to tell if these two rocks are the same one. No new ideas were coming to either one.

"I'm going to touch it," says Chris, breaking the silence.

"Are you sure that is a good idea?" April asks, concerned.

"I want to see what happens."

"Chris, I'm not too sure about this."

"April, the stories I've been told about my rock is when you touch it, it will give an electrical shock. I want to see how bad the shock is."

"I've heard the same stories here. Just…be careful."

"I am."

Chris waves his hand above the rock. The glassy black surface with his hand reflecting on the surface does not do anything. No lightning bolts light up, definitely no thunder boom.

"Here I go," Chris says and places his bare hand on the rock's surface. He feels an instant tingling sensation go through his hand and up his arm to his elbow. He pulls his hand away before it goes any higher.

"That wasn't too bad," he says. "You try it, April. See what you think."

"Oh, I don't know," April says, reluctantly.

"It's just a tingling sensation. You're not going to be electrocuted."

"It doesn't hurt?" she asks.

"Not at all. Try it."

"Okay, here I go."

Chris puts his hand back on the rock too.

"Do you feel it?" he asks. "Kind of tickles, doesn't it?"

"It does. It feels kind of funny. It feels like when you hit your funny bone," April says, giggling.

"I have taken my hand off, April."

"Me too. My hand is off. The tingle goes away just like that, huh."

"I guess so. Hey, why don't you go find a bathroom, and I'll stay with my rock and try to figure out something we can do to determine if these rocks are the same."

"Okay. My hotel is a few blocks from here. That's where I'll go."

"Sounds good. Hurry back."

"Chris!" April shouts. "I can't move!"

"What do you mean you can't move?" Chris asks.

"I'm trying to move, but my legs won't go," she answers, panicking.

Chris climbs up the ladder onto the walkway. He takes two steps and turns back to look down at the rock.

April says, "Okay, I just took two steps forward and turned. I didn't want to turn. Now, I'm stuck, again."

"I took two steps and turned. I'm leaning on the handrail, looking down at this rock," Chris says.

"Chris, what's going on?"

"I don't know, April. You said you moved the same as I did? Let's try something and see if we do it again. I'm going to turn and take one step. Tell me what you do. Ready. Here I go."

"I turned ninety degrees and took one step," April says, still panicking. "Chris, *what is going on?*"

"I think we are connected, somehow. When we touched the rock at the same time, it connected us. It's like we are magnetized to each other," Chris replies, looking around the basement. He looks at the front wall where the man rammed into it repeatedly. This would explain that story, he thinks.

"How, Chris? What is happening?" April asks. "I don't like this. What are we going to do?"

"I'm not sure. This is my first time being a magnet."

"This isn't funny, Chris." She snaps at him.

"It kind of is, but let's make sure this is what I'm thinking it is. I'm going to take a step in the direction I think is west. I need you to tell me if you go east. If so, then we will definitely know we are magnetized together. Ready and step."

"Chris, I turned a little bit and stepped."

"What direction are you facing?"

"Um, east. Yeah, I'm going east. I remember the sun set over there, behind me."

"April, do you know what this means?" Chris asks, smiling and excited.

"Yeah, Chris, it means I can't move unless you move."

"Well, yeah, there is that, but we just proved these two rocks are the same. Your theory is correct. This rock is an antipode. I think some excitement is in order. We did it."

"Oh, my God, Chris. We did. We proved it." April clapped her hands together and did a fist pump over her head. "Wow, we really did it. Not to be a Debbie Downer, though, but we still have this movement problem."

"Yeah, we have been magnetized, somehow."

"So what do we do?" April asks. "I really have to pee." She stresses.

"We are going to have to work together until we can figure out how to break the magnetism. We are going to have to stay in line with each other. If we do get out of line, the magnetism will snatch us back in line. Right now, April, we are two magnets connected to each other, somehow."

"So again, I ask, what are we going to do?"

"We will have to go together," Chris answers.

"I can't pee with you with me."

"I'll be here in Argentina. You'll get to pee by yourself. We'll have to work together to get you to a bathroom, unless there is a porta-potty close to you that you might consider using."

"Absolutely not. They are dirty, and they stink. You know this. They're just some things I am not going to do."

"Okay. Just asking." Chris laughs out loud.

"Quit laughing. You know me and my quirks. So what is the plan? I'm about to take off running, and you will just have to keep up," April says as she starts to dance.

"First things first, I have to get out of this basement. Once I get out of here, you can take off running, if you must, although I would prefer we walk," Chris replies.

"Okay, but we really need to hurry, please."

"April, I'm going to walk toward the stairs. They're west of me. Can you walk east fairly, easily?"

"I can. I should be able to go about fifty yards to the fence," April answers.

"I don't have to go too far. Maybe about fifty feet. Are you ready?"

"Yes!" April exclaimed. "Please, don't go too fast. I have my walking shoes on, but the ground is uneven in places."

"I'm not. Here we go and begin."

Chris walks across the basement. April walks across the construction site ground.

"All right, April, I'm at the stairs. I'm turning and starting up."

"I'm turning and walking too." A thought comes to April as she walks, and she starts laughing. She tells Chris. "I just had a funny thought. I'm glad I'm not high stepping like I'm climbing stairs. That would be embarrassing."

Chris chuckles at the vision of April high stepping across flat ground and says, "I'm at the top."

"Okay," April says, smiling because she heard Chris laugh at her thought.

"April, I have to go back across the cathedral to the front doors. I'll be going east. About how far are you going to have to go to get out of the construction site?"

"I will need to go about sixty yards to the fence in a straight line. If I go diagonally toward the gate, about seventy yards, can you go diagonally?"

"I will have to go straight until I get outside," Chris answers.

"Okay."

They start walking, Chris in the main hall of the cathedral and April across the construction site. Chris approaches Sister Cortez's office doorway where she has appeared, looking curiously at him.

Sister Cortez asks, "Mr. Collier, is everything all right? Did you find the answer you needed?"

"Yes, ma'am, we did," Chris answers, slowing his walking pace.

"What are you doing?" April asks. "Why are you slowing down? You're not going to stop and talk, are you? I swear, I'll start running if you do."

"I'm still going. Didn't want to be rude," Chris says, placing his hand over his mouth and mouthpiece.

Sister Cortez asks, "So is it the same rock as the one your partner has in Hong Kong, Mr. Collier?" She looks at him, expecting him to stop and talk with her.

Chris looks at Sister Cortez, smiling, as he keeps walking. He says, "Yes, it is the same rock. Um, Sister Cortez, I'm sorry, I can't stop and talk right now. We are in a bit of a situation, my partner and I." He turns back to face Sister Cortez. Walking backward, he continues, "My partner has to pee real bad, and I'm helping her get to the bathroom right now."

"Chris!" April shouts. "Are you gonna tell everyone?"

Chris tells April, "Sorry." Back to Sister Cortez, "I promise, I'll come back, later, I hope, and I'll tell you what we found out. Okay? She really has to go, so, uh—"

"*Chris!*" April screams. "Oh, my God."

Sister Cortez watches Chris walk backward with her eyes narrow. She says, "Mr. Collier, I don't understand. She has to use the restroom, and you are helping her get to one. I thought you said she is in Hong Kong?"

Chris smiles and says, "She is. Uh, Sister Cortez, you know the story about the guy who touched the rock and then walked into the wall several times?"

"Yes, I'm familiar with it. I told you I was." She retorted.

"Sister Cortez, we now know what caused him to do that."

April says into the phone, "What are you talking about? We now know why who did what?"

"I'll tell you about it, later," Chris says to April. Back to Sister Cortez. "I promise I will come back and tell you everything. I'm not trying to be rude, but she has to go, badly, and I do have to help her."

April laughs and says, "I'm not dying yet."

"I am."

Sister Cortez gave Chris a puzzled look and says in Spanish, "People get stranger by the minute." To Chris, she says, "Yes, please come back and tell me what you have discovered about that rock. The elders are very interested."

Chris waved to her and turned around just as he arrived at the front doors.

Outside Iglesia Nuestra Señora del Perpetuo Sucorro, Chris squints his eyes as the sunshine seems brighter. His eyes adjusting, he descends the stairs down to the sidewalk. He says to April, "I'm going to continue straight until I get across the street to the park."

"Okay. Probably about another thirty yards, and I'll be at the fence."

They are both quiet while Chris crosses the street. April is really feeling the pressure on her bladder. She is about ten yards from the fence. She suddenly turns left and trips on a small rock, rolls her ankle, and falls to the ground.

"What happened?" she asks, rolling over and sitting up. She moves her foot in a circular motion testing her ankle.

Chris is stopped with one foot still in the air, waiting to be placed on the ground so it can continue with the other foot.

"What happened, April? I've stopped."

"I tripped and fell," April says, standing up and dusting herself. "I'm guessing you have a reason for making that sudden move?"

"Yeah. I was about to walk into a tree. Are you okay?"

"I'm fine. That didn't help my bladder much. You need to say something before you move like that. You could have hurt me."

"I'm so sorry. My mind wondered on me. I was looking around this park, when the tree jumped out in front of me," Chris says, with a hint of a smile creeping into the corners of his mouth.

"Eyes forward, Chris. Pay attention to the task at hand. Do you hear me. Keep your eyes forward," April says, perturbed. "I'm going to turn left and go to the gate now."

"Okay, you lead the way, and again, I'm sorry."

"Just stay in line and no more sudden moves please," she states.

"Yes, ma'am. You said your hotel is how far from the site?"

"It's a couple of blocks."

"Is it in a straight line, or do we have to make turns?"

"It's straight ahead. When I go through the gate, I'll go left a little to the sidewalk, and then, it's a straight shot up the sidewalk. I'm going through the gate now. Let me lock it."

Chris asks, "Are you locked and ready?"

"Yes. Let's go."

"How far is the sidewalk?"

"About ten feet."

"Can you go right or left a couple of feet?"

"I can't go right. There is a building, and the fence is on my left. It's a narrow walkway. Why? Is something wrong?"

"Yeah," he says, drawing out the yeah. "I'm about to come upon a park bench. If you could go a little in either direction, I wouldn't have to climb over it."

"I can go left a little, not much."

"That would be fine. A little more."

"I'm against the fence, now. Chris, I'm beginning to think you are trying to embarrass me on purpose."

"No, I figured it would look normal if I walked around it. Are you trying to embarrass me?"

"No, but it does seem like you have a lot of obstacles in your way."

"I'm following you," he says, laughing.

April is on the sidewalk. Chris is almost to the other side of the park.

April asks, "Are you going to be able to walk in a straight line the rest of the way?"

"Well, there is a building directly in front of me."

"Oh, nice," she states. "Is it open?"

"No, it's boarded up."

"Oh, come on. Really?"

"I do see an alley to my right. It's about ten or twelve steps away."

"That far?"

"You sound worried."

"Yes, I am. Let's go, before I go here."

"That sounds like a good idea. Go right there," Chris suggested.

"Chris, no."

April moves on her sidewalk. Chris exits the park and crosses the street in front of the boarded-up building.

Chris says, "Stop. I'm at the building. I'm going to need to go about ten steps right."

"Chris, that's going to put me in the street."

"Well…watch out for traffic."

"Uh." April gasps.

"I've have to get to the alley, dear."

"Ugh. Okay. Go." April exasperates, looking both ways before stepping into the street.

"All right, I'm here at the entrance."

Looking down the alley for any obstacles or problems that may hinder his progress, he spots one and shakes his head from side to side and curses quietly; the fence is about thirty yards into the alley going across from building to building.

April hears Chris mumbling and asks, "So how does it look? Are you going to be able to go through the alley?"

Chris answers, "Yeah, I can get through. I'm going to have to climb a fence."

"Oh, good grief. Well, shall we proceed?" April asks, rolling her eyes.

Starting into the alley and eyeing the fence directly in front of him, he sees that the fence is a basic chain link-style fence. He does not see any electrical wires or barb wire attached to it. He sighs in relief just as another thought comes to him. What if there is a dog or a group of dogs on the other side? The fence has strips of plastic woven into it to keep people from looking through it. He shrugs his shoulders. He thinks there is nothing I can do about it. Hopefully, they are nice dogs. He walks on.

April shouts, "*Car!*"

Chris is turned and slammed into the wall of the building on his left.

April is stopped short of the sidewalk she is dashing toward to get out of the road. She needs about two more steps to the sidewalk and safety. The car approaching in the lane she is standing blows his horn as he stops a few feet from her. He is not able to swerve around her because another car is approaching from the opposite lane. The driver of the car in the outside lane is turned, staring at April standing in the road not trying to move onto the sidewalk and out of the way. He drives past. The car that has stopped and blown his horn at her is now yelling at her in Chinese.

April stares straight ahead at the sidewalk she cannot move to get to, embarrassed about her situation. She does not dare look at the driver yelling at her.

The car veers around her, blows his horn one more time, and drives off. April starts to breathe again. She asks, "What happened?"

"I hit a wall. Hard," Chris answers.

"Oh, my gosh. Are you okay? I had to hurry out of the way for a car coming at me, and there was another one coming the other way."

"I don't think I broke anything. Maybe a couple of teeth were knocked out. I'll know for sure when I get feeling back in my body," Chris replies.

April began feeling flustered. "We have got to figure out how to break this magnetism. This is ridiculous."

"Well, you could keep slamming me up against the wall. That would eventually disrupt the magnetism."

"Chris, I'm serious."

"I am too. Beating a magnet with something hard like a hammer, or, in our case, a wall, will disrupt the magnetic charge. That is probably how the guy in the basement of the cathedral broke his magnetism. He hit the wall several times, very hard."

"What guy?" April asks, curious.

"It's the story the lady I met this morning told me. It's the reason why it is so hard to get to the rock at the cathedral. I'll tell it to you later," Chris says.

"You said he hit the wall several times?" April asks, astonished. "Chris, do you really want to be slammed into a wall repeatedly?"

"Not really," Chris replies. "But I do want to see if the one hit I just took has freed us. Try to take a step."

"All right, here I go. Nope. I still can't move."

"Oh, well. You're still in the street?"

"Yeah"

"Okay, I'll get up off the ground now. I guess you didn't slam me hard enough to break us apart."

"I'll try harder next time." April laughed. "What are we going to do about this? We can't stay like this, forever."

Chris replies. "Maybe it will eventually wear off. I have been trying to figure out how we have been magnetized together. I mean, the human body is made up of mostly water, and water doesn't magnetize. What are your thoughts on this?"

"Maybe it's the fillings in our teeth, or oh, I don't know."

"I thought that too. But the guy in the basement at the cathedral. That was over a hundred years ago. Metal fillings weren't around then. I guess this is just way too far over our heads. Shall we proceed onward? I'm about five yards from the fence."

They both move forward. He tells her he is at the fence, and he climbs up to look over it.

April says, "I am just about at my hotel. Can you make it beyond the fence?"

"Yeah," answers Chris. "There is a dumpster up against the fence. It looks like it spreads out into a big lot back here."

He climbs over the fence onto the dumpster and down to the ground. He walks into the open lot.

April arrives at her hotel.

"I've got to turn right." She enters the lobby. Chris tells her he is good and that he has plenty of room. April asks, "Um, what's going to happen when I get on the elevator and go up?"

"Well, hopefully, I don't get squashed into the ground, but other than that, I don't know."

"I'm at the elevator. The doors are open. I'm stepping on it. The doors are closing."

Chris hears a blip on his headset. He has lost signal with April. After a few seconds, his phone rings. He answers.

"Hey, I lost signal when I got on the elevator. I'm on my way to my room now," April says.

"You're walking, April?"

"Yeah, aren't you?"

"No. I'm standing still," he answers.

April asks, "Did we break the magnetism? How did we do that?"

Chris claps his hands together and answers, "Of course, the elevators have a magnetic field. If they are in the center of the building, they put out a magnetic field. That disrupted the magnetism that was holding us together."

April shouts out, "Happy days! We are free!"

Chris replies to her sarcastically, "What, you didn't like being stuck with me?"

April giggles and says, "Chris, I have got to pee. I'll call you later. Bye."

Chapter 6

Chris wraps his headset around his neck. He looks around at the backlot of the two buildings he is standing behind. To comprehend what has happened to him and April is way beyond his means. He has always been convinced that magical powers do not exist; at least in the real world, they do not exist.

How did what just happened to April and I, happen? We were magnetized. We could not move without the other. She is on the other side of the world. If I remember correctly from reading all those useless information trivia books, the Earth's circumference is just under twenty-five thousand miles. That amounts to a lot of area between April and I, and the Earth is definitely not hollow. Everybody knows that.

He is perplexed. Walking back to the alley, climbing the dumpster and fence, and walking through the alley back to the park, the question of how "what just happened" hangs over him, bothering him to no end. Who can explain it?

He sits down on one of the park benches. He looks across the park at the cathedral. He observes the old bricks that make up the exterior of the cathedral. He works his eyes up to the clock that is below the steeple. It shows the current time of day. He is still absolutely dumbfounded. Where is the answer to the question? It is obviously not on the outside of the cathedral.

Under that cathedral is a rock. A rock that is blacker than the blackest blacks, with a surface that is as smooth as glass, a surface that cannot be scratched. It goes all the way through the Earth. It is a rebar. It holds the Earth together, just like the rebar that is put into concrete. The rock begins or ends here in La Quiaca, Argentina. It literally goes all the way to Hong Kong, China, where it begins or ends there. And it has unexplainable powers, the power to magnetize two people together, who are a world apart.

Chris focuses his stare at the ground in front of him. He shakes his head side to side and says to no one, "Don't ever think you have seen it all, because if you do, something like this will happen."

A shadow approaches him followed by Sister Cortez. "Mr. Collier, are you all right? You look as pale as a ghost. Can I get you something? A water perhaps?"

"Oh, uh, hey, Sister Cortez," Chris says, startled. "Thank you, I'm fine. I'm trying to solve a mystery."

"May I sit with you?"

"Yes, please." He pats the bench next to him. "I'm sorry to have worried you. I've been lost in thought. I was witness, or I believe I should say, a participant in a moment I'm not sure I believe happened."

"That's interesting. Is it in relation to the black diamond? You did say that this rock here is the same as the rock your partner has in Hong Kong?"

"Yes, ma'am, to both questions," Chris answers, smiling at her.

"That is magnificent." Sister Cortez is delighted.

"Yes, ma'am. It is absolutely magnificent. Hard to believe what happened, but yes, it is the real deal."

"Tell me about what happened. How did you and your partner discover the two were the same rock?" she asks.

Chris turns to face her and laughs. "We touched them at the same time."

"Oh," she says, surprised. "What happened when you two touched them?"

"That is the mystery. Amazingly, the rock connected us together, somehow."

"How do you mean? It connected the two of you? I don't under-stand, Mr. Collier."

"I don't understand it either. We touched the rock at the same time with no gloves on, and when we let go, neither one of us could move. I tried to move, and when I did, she moved. We finally figured out that we were magnetized together. We had to stay in a straight line with each other. That's why I couldn't stop to talk with you earlier. She really did have to go to the bathroom, and in order for her to get there, I had to go with her. If I stopped, then she would have stopped."

"That's very interesting." She looks at him puzzled.

"It is. I've been trying to figure it out. I know you probably thought I was crazy, earlier, but it really did happen. I don't know how, but it did."

"I did think you had weirded out. Anyway, are you two still connected?"

"No. She made it to her hotel, and when she got on the elevator, it demagnetized us. The elevators have a magnetic field around them. That disrupted the magnetism."

"That is fascinating. You think that might have been what happened to that man so many years ago, who hit the wall in the basement? Somebody touched the rock at the same time he did."

"It does make a lot of sense now, Sister Cortez. He hit the wall harder and harder each time until they broke the magnetism."

"This is absolutely fascinating. Two people a world apart connected together. I'm going to have a hard time explaining that to the elders. Could you help me?" Sister Cortez asks Chris.

Chris and Sister Cortez talk about the events of the morning into the afternoon.

April comes out of her bathroom feeling relieved she made it and excited about the discovery her and Chris made. She opens the curtains in her room, sits down in a room chair, and reflects back to earlier. She ignores the Hong Kong night outside her window as she retraces each sequence of events that happened. She logs every detail into her laptop.

After double-checking what she entered into her laptop, she grabs her phone off the bed and calls Tom Henderson.

"The rocks are the same rock." She nearly shouts into the phone after Tom answers.

"You're certain?" Tom asks back.

"Yes, I am certain. One hundred percent certain, Tom. They are the same rock."

"Wonderful, absolutely wonderful news, April. I have to ask though. How in the world did you two match them together?"

"We touched them at the same time," April answers and begins to explain to Tom the events of the night. She tells him everything that happened after they touched the rock. She asks Tom if he knew the answer to why they were magnetized together. He does not know right off, but he says he will find out the answer and let her know. This puzzles Tom as he listens to April. He writes a note down to remind him to ask the scientist to really study this rock. *This thing is magnetizing people? How? What is this rock?*

April and Tom talk for a good hour, trying to comprehend what happened.

Tom says to April after their conversation slowed down, "You need to get to Honolulu and check out the rock that has been found there. Find where the other side could be and send Chris there."

"I will. I'll leave not this morning, but the next morning. I'll talk to Chris. Hopefully, he'll help me with this rock too."

"Surely, he will. He's excited about this too."

"He is. It's the fact that he is using his own money. Another long trip is going to be expensive. I don't know if he will do another one. Have you talked to the Board about reimbursing him for this trip? I told him I would repay him, but I don't know if and when I'll be able to."

"I'll ask them again, April." Tom lies. "With this discovery you two made, they should repay him. Look, April, I'll see you in Honolulu."

"You're still going to be there?" she asks, hoping he did not hear the dread in her tone.

"I'm already here, dear. I'm waiting for you."

"Oh, really?" April wants to cry or scream or both. She begins pacing around her room. She needs to throw something.

"Yes. I'm sitting outside on the balcony of our hotel watching the scenery right now."

He means watching women in their swimsuits on the beach, April thinks.

"Well then, I guess I'll see you soon."

She hangs up her phone and lays down on her bed. After a minute of staring at the ceiling, she turns over and buries her face in the pillow and screams. She curses Tom for a moment, and after letting all of her hate for him out, she relaxes and falls asleep.

Chapter 7

April wakes at four in the morning in Hong Kong. She takes a shower and dresses and fixes herself a cup of coffee. Taking a seat in a chair by the window, she powers up her laptop and books a flight to Honolulu at nine o'clock.

After finishing with her flight booking, she begins the task of gathering information on the rock in Honolulu. She needs to find the antipode from the exact location of the rock in Honolulu and pinpoint the exact spot on the other side of Earth that the other end of the rock should be. Using her formula and longitude and latitude lines, she is very excited to learn that the rock would be on dry land and not on the bottom of the ocean. The location of the rock is a concern to her because the information shows it being in Botswana, Africa, out in the middle of nowhere in the Chobe National Park. She looks up the average temperature for that region and sees that during the summer months, the temperature can reach a consistent one hundred and twenty degrees during the daylight hours.

April works on gathering information and relaying information to the scientist who had come to Hong Kong for this rock right up until it is time for her to check out of the hotel and go to the airport. She would call Chris from the plane. She hopes he would be game for another adventure and help her with this new rock. She knows this is going to take some serious coaxing on her part to get him to do another one, and this trip would probably be a lot more expensive than the trip down to Argentina. She closes her eyes and lays her head back in the cab's back seat. She is worried about Chris and what he would say.

Her plane takes off from Hong Kong, and after leveling off and getting to the correct altitude, the flight attendant informs the passengers that they may move about freely and use their electronic devices. She picks up her phone, takes a deep breath, and punches Chris's name on her phone screen.

"Chris, hey, how are you?" she says apprehensively, after he answered.

"I'm good," he answers and then asks, "What happened to you? I was expecting to hear from you a lot sooner than this. I thought I was abandoned."

"I went to bed after I used the bathroom. I was tired. What have you been doing?"

He answers, "Well, I talked with Sister Cortez from the cathedral for a while telling her about our adventure and what we found out about the rock, you know, the magical power of it. Now, I'm here in my room. I just finished eating and was actually about to call you before I left. So tell me, have you told everyone what we discovered?"

"I have," she answers.

"Were they excited? Are we going to be famous? What's the story?" Chris asks, curious.

April replies, "They are very excited. They are sending people here and there to do more studies on our rock. As for the fame thing, I don't know about that. They did, however, request us to check out another rock. So do I need to ask, or are you game for another one?"

"Another one?" Chris exacerbated. "You mean there are more of these rocks?"

"Yes," April answers. "There is another one. Same makeup as this rock. Will not break, can't scratch the surface, and believe me, from what I was told, they really tried to scratch it up. They hit it with a ditch-digging machine. They found it while we were working on this rock. Kind of ironic, I think."

"I'm guessing the ditch-digging machine didn't fare too well when it hit the rock?"

"From the picture I received, it totaled it," April says.

"I imagine that scared everyone around too. Anyway, where is this new rock located?" Chris wonders.

"It's in Honolulu," she says.

"Honolulu, huh? That sounds cool. I've never been there either. I'll get my stuff together and start making my way to Hawaii. Where is your side located, April?"

"Chris, I'm sorry. I'm going to Honolulu. In fact, I'm on my way now."

"Oh…well." Chris is stunned by what she said. She's already on her way. "So I'm guessing you have a far-off, remote place that is directly opposite of Honolulu for me to go to."

"Does this mean you will definitely do another one?" she asks, hoping he would.

"Well, April, that depends on where you are going to send me. I don't think I need to tell you, this trip was not cheap. Have you found out anything about me being reimbursed for this trip?"

"Please, Chris. I really need you for this," April pleads.

"I understand, April. But wherever it is you are wanting me to go from here is sounding like it is going to be a long way away. That's going to cost a lot of money out of my pocket. I need to know for sure that I will be repaid. Send me a confirmation note from someone that is in charge of this expedition that says I will be reimbursed for this trip. Then, we can discuss the next one."

"I promise you, Chris, I am working on getting you repaid."

"I believe you, April. But I still need some kind of confirmation. Or how about I go to Hawaii since it is closer to Argentina than Hong Kong, and you go wherever the other end is. Economically, that would be the wisest choice."

"Chris, I understand your point, but I have to be in Hawaii. There are going to be some people there that I have to talk with. I have to show them what we found out."

"I thought you said there were people in Hong Kong and people on their way here. Who else do you have to talk with?"

"There are a lot of people interested in this, Chris. And they are going to want to know, right off, if you are going to help with this new rock. Will you help me?" April feels her stomach knotting up. She totally understands Chris's point of view. She just cannot make herself tell Chris that Tom Henderson is the only person waiting for her in Honolulu.

"I can talk to them, April, or better yet, we can talk to them together. How about that?"

"Chris, I need you on the other side," April states, calmly. "When I get to Hawaii, I will tell them you must be reimbursed your money. I promise."

"April, I'm going to need confirmation before I go anywhere. Call me back before you send it to me." Chris hangs up his phone.

April is stunned. She stares at her phone's wallpaper for a moment and then looks out the window of the plane. She never knew Chris to get worked up like he did. She understands where he was coming from. This next trip is going to be very expensive. She, also, knows that getting him his money back is going to be a challenge. It hurt her, sitting here, helpless, that she is probably going to do something that she would regret.

Chris goes to bed shortly after talking with April. He packs up his bag and is ready to leave for home when he realizes it was too late to leave. He would go in the morning.

April calls Tom after calming down and drying her eyes. She hopes Tom would not hear in her voice that she had been crying.

"Hey, sweetie," Tom Henderson says, answering on the first ring.

"Hello," April replies back, rolling her eyes. "We have a problem. Chris will not go to the next rock until he gets a guarantee in writing that he will be reimbursed for this trip."

"Did you tell him he would be paid in full after the second rock is finished?"

"Is he going to be, Tom? Have you talked with the Board about this issue?"

"I'm working on it." Tom lies. "I've told them that Chris is assisting with the discovery. They said they would add him to the budget."

"Well, could you get someone from the Board to send him an email stating that he will be reimbursed one hundred percent of his money?" April asks, trying not to sound whiny.

"Tell you what, dear, I will tell him myself," Tom says, with a bit of evilness in his tone.

"I don't know if that will work. He made it clear he wanted an official confirmation."

"April, I will have a confirmation note sent to him by the time you get here. I know exactly who to call. Will that work for you?"

"Yes, it will, Tom. Please make it work. I want him to get all his money back."

"I will make the call right now. See you soon."

April texts Chris that he should be receiving an email from the Board anytime. She gets no response back.

Chris leaves the hotel in La Quiaca at eight in the morning. He finds the friend with a truck that he rode into town with sitting outside the restaurant down the street from the hotel. As he approaches the truck, he looks at the rims to see if he puts the lugs back on. He has, and he smiles when he sees Chris. Chris asks him if he could catch a ride back to the airport with him. The friend with a truck keeps smiling and points to the bed of the truck. Chris hops in and sits down on the floor. After about ten minutes, the truck cranks up when the friend with a truck friend comes out of the restaurant carrying a bag full of food. Some words are exchanged between the two in the cab followed by some laughter, and they are off.

Chris stretches his legs out and leans back against the bedrail. He takes his phone out of its holster and reads April's text again. There is still no email from the Board. He thinks about calling her but decides against it for now. He is considering going ahead and doing the other rock and then demanding his money back when he comes face to face with whomever is in charge. But reasoning kicks in, and he is a business person, so he decides to wait for a confirmation.

The truck stops in front of the Aeropuerto La Quiaca. Chris jumps out of the bed of the truck and stops at the passenger side door. He thanks the friend with a truck, shakes both guys' hand, and enters the terminal.

The plane is due to arrive in about an hour, so Chris takes a seat in the waiting area. His phone starts ringing just as he dozes off. It is April.

"Hi there," he says. "How are you?"

"I'm good. How about you?"

"Can't complain. I'm about to leave this hole in the world. Things are starting to look up. I haven't received any emails from the Board, if that is what you were calling about."

"I know. We are here working on it. I, personally, wanted you to know that I will get you reimbursed. It might take a little more time than I thought it would, but I promise, you will get your money back. I give you my word as a friend. Where are you anyway?"

"I'm at the Aeropuerto La Quiaca. My plane will be here soon, I hope. How is Honolulu? You are there now, aren't you?"

"Yes, I'm here. Tom Henderson is here too."

"Oh, well." Chris is stunned by this information. "Are you two going to be working together on this new rock or what?"

"He's going to be involved with it. I was hoping you would help also. I really need you."

"April, I would love to," Chris says, facetiously, "but the expense of it is going to knock a big hole in my money. That's money I need for my business and for retirement someday. You see where I'm coming from. I would love to, but I need assurance."

"I understand. Is my word not good enough? I promise, if it is the last thing I ever do, you will get your money back. All of it!"

"April," he says, running his hand over his head, "can you tell me where the other side of the rock is?"

"Does this mean you will go?"

"No. It means 'where is the other side of the rock?'"

"Botswana, Africa."

"Holy cow, April. That's going to be a mighty trip."

"Will you go and do this with me, Chris? Please."

Chris puts his head down in his hand. He thinks about what he would do when he gets home. He thinks about her and what she means to him.

Finally, he answers her, "Yes, I will do it for you."

"Thank you so much." She almost cries.

"You bet. Send me the information I'll need."

"I'll text it to you now. Thank you. I'll keep my word."

"I know you will. My plane is here. I'll be in touch with you soon."

"Okay. Chris, please be careful."

"I will. Bye."

"Bye."

April set her phone down and looks over at Tom. She says to him, "You better get him his money." She gets up and walks away.

Chris climbs aboard the same plane that brought him to La Quiaca. The same pilot smiles at him and shakes his hand. He already dreads this new trip.

Chapter 8

Chris arrives in Johannesburg two full days after leaving La Quiaca, Argentina. The first leg of his trip, the flight from La Quiaca to Buenos Aires, scared him to the point that he almost grabbed a parachute and jumped out of the plane. A thunderstorm rolled in on them and the wind that came with the storm had the plane jumping up and down. At one time during the flight, Chris swore they were pointed directly at the ground. The pilot took it all in stride. He said to Chris while he, too, was squinting to see through the front windshield that he had flown through worse than this. Chris did not doubt him. He just hoped the pilot could make it through this one.

The storm lasted all of thirty minutes, and once they made it out the backside, the flight was smooth all the way into Buenos Aires. The flights from Buenos Aires all the way to Johannesburg were much smoother and nicer being that they were on much larger planes. When he exited the plane at the airport in Johannesburg, he was still questioning his mortality and debating on whether it was too late for him to find religion.

Chris grabs his bag from the luggage carousel and meanders down the concourse looking for the auto rental counter. He rents a jeep on the last leg of this trip. He spots the rental company's sign and approaches the counter. After a little flirting from him and the girl behind the counter, he makes his way outside and waits for the courtesy valet to bring him his jeep.

After getting directions to the nearest sporting goods store from the valet, Chris exits the airport and begins the search for the store. He wants to go ahead and get his supplies for the trip now because when he gets to his hotel, which he just passed, he is going straight to shower, eat, and then bed. He is absolutely worn out. He knows pretty much what he is going to need for his trip to the middle of nowhere Botswana. He researches the area where the Honolulu rock is supposed to come through on the middle leg of his flight.

Geared up, Chris finds a fast-food restaurant and proceeds to his hotel. His plan is to get to bed early so he can be up before the sun rises. He has a good eight-hour drive ahead of him to get to the site.

All settled in, Chris calls April.

April answers her phone on the second ring. "Chris, hey, thank God. I was really getting worried about you. Where are you?"

"Hey, April," Chris replies, yawning. "I'm in Johannesburg. I'm just calling to check in with you and let you know I'm still alive. I'm about to go to bed."

"Oh, okay. How was the trip?" She already knows the answer but asks it anyway.

"Long," Chris answers. "It took two days to get here."

"Oh!" April exclaims, shocked.

"Yeah. Well, like I said, I just wanted to check in with you. I'm going to get some sleep. My plan is to leave out really early and drive up to the site."

"Okay, Chris. Thank you. I'll talk to you later."

Chris ends the call on his phone and turns out the bedside light. He falls asleep in ten seconds.

April places her phone down next to her cup of coffee at the table she and Tom sat at eating breakfast. She had arrived in Honolulu from Hong Kong the morning before. When she arrived in Honolulu, Tom came to the airport to pick her up. He took her back to the hotel and took her to his room. April entered his room with a disgusted look on her face. She was so tired from the trip and everything that had happened in Hong Kong, she totally forgot to check for a room of her own. She placed her bag down on the luggage rack, opened it, grabbed some clean clothes and toiletries, and went to the bathroom for a shower. She did not say a word to Tom. After showering, she dressed and went straight to bed. She got situated under the covers, and then she looked over at Tom, who was sitting in a chair looking out the window. He turned to watch her climb into bed. He had a sad look on his face when he realized her intention was to go to sleep.

April looked at him and said, "I'll be getting my own room when I wake up." She was sound asleep in no time. Tom stared at her for a long time. He had really hoped she had missed him so much that she was desperately in need of some attention. He knew he sure was in need. He watched her sleep for a minute, then returned to his window watching. He was bothered by her abruptness with him, but he figured she was just tired.

April slept most of the first day in Honolulu. She did secure herself a room after she woke up, leaving Tom's room without saying goodbye.

April decides that she, at least, needs to be copacetic with Tom, so here she is having breakfast with him. She looks across the table at Tom after setting her phone down and says, "Chris is in Johannesburg."

Tom replies, "That's good. When will he be leaving for the rock?"

"He said he is going to get up real early and drive to it on his morning. Now, back to my question. What have you found out about reimbursing Chris for his expenses?"

Tom looks across at the table at April. He puts his hands up in defense and shakes his head side to side. He says, "They said they wouldn't be able to reimburse him, it's not in the budget. They only budgeted for one person, and that is you."

"You knew this was going to be a two-person job. There is no way one person could do it." April is furious. "Tom, the trip from Argentina to Johannesburg, by itself, probably costs close to six thousand dollars, plus the cost of the trip from Birmingham to Argentina. And he has to get back home."

"I'm sorry, April. To be honest with you, this discovery wasn't supposed to happen. They wanted to send you out on a field assignment to see how you would do with researching. They had hoped you would have called someone local in that town in Argentina and used them for the possible discovery."

April stares at Tom. "You mean they didn't know about Chris?"

"Not until after the discovery was confirmed by you two."

April swallows her coffee hard. "You said I could use Chris, if he would do it. You said that would be fine." She leans back in her chair, her mouth shaped in an "O." "You didn't say anything to the Board about Chris, did you?"

"April, again, I'm sorry. We really didn't think this was going to happen. All we can do for Chris is thank him for his contribution to this historical discovery."

Very angry by the revelation Tom has just let be known, April leans her hands against the table and shouts quietly at Tom. "I am going to go to my room now and get ready for my Chris to call. We are going to find out if this rock here in Honolulu is the antipode to the rock in Botswana. If you and your so-called friends on the Board want to know what we find out, Chris better be reimbursed for every penny he has spent on this assignment. If he is not, I will quit my job and tell everybody who will listen that this was just a hoax and that you and The National Board of Geography conspired together to garner some attention."

"April, they know about the Hong Kong/Argentina rock. Scientists and archeologists are already at the two sites gathering information and studying."

"Who's paying their expenses?" April spats.

"I don't know. The government, I guess."

"Get on the phone with them, and get Chris his money. I'm serious, Tom," April says with very wide, angry eyes.

Tom cowards back in his chair. "I'll see what I can do. I'm not promising anything, April."

"Well, then, how about you pay him out of your pocket!"

"I can't do that. You know what I make."

"After these discoveries, you will be rich and famous." She hissed.

"So will you and Chris." Tom shoots back.

"Oh, you'll find a way to leave him out!" And with that remark, April storms off.

Chapter 9

Leaving Johannesburg well before the sun came up is a great idea. Chris has the windows down on his rental jeep. The cool morning air feels great blowing into the interior. Once the sun comes up though, it's a different story. With no air conditioning in the jeep, he is already on his third bottle of ice-cold water, and he is drenched in sweat by the time he makes it to the halfway point of his trip to the rock in Botswana. The landscape on either side of the road looks dry as a bone as he rides by, with no relief in sight. He visualizes the vegetation watching him drink from his water bottle as he drives by and giving him the dirtiest of looks for not stopping and sharing with them. He swears at one time, he thinks he sees a bush coming after him. The heat is absolutely brutal.

His memory of driving in heat like this when he started in the trucking business comes vividly back to him. The old truck that he started out with had no air conditioner. He could not afford to get it fixed. He would drive across west Texas, the Arizona desert, and it always happened in the summer. How he remembered those days, keeping a handkerchief in his lap to wipe his brow, his water jug never staying cold for long, and his clothes sticking to his body. At the end of the day, he would take his boots off and literally pour sweat water out of them.

Those memories of the past keeps his mind occupied as he drives. Those were the days that separated the men from the boys. Today's truckers have it easy, air conditioning, automatic shifter, refrigerators in the sleeper, microwaves, TV, and about all the amenities of home.

Chris looks at the dash at his GPS screen. The GPS tells him he has thirty minutes until he will arrive at his destination. He calls April to make sure she is awake and ready to do this.

"Hello," answers the sleepy voice of April Mckenzie.

"Did I wake you?" Chris asks with a chuckle.

"Yeah," she answers. "Are you there?"

"Will be in less than thirty minutes."

"Okay," she yawns. "I'll get my stuff and go down to my rock. Why didn't you call earlier? I would have been ready and waiting."

"There's no hurry, is there? Besides, I've been enjoying my drive, except the heat. Haven't enjoyed that too much. It gets hot here early, and it doesn't let up. Of course, I could have splurged and gotten a ride with air conditioning, but I'm no sissy. It's two in the afternoon here, and I've already drank a gallon of water. I'm okay."

"Aren't you just a tough guy," April says. "It's three in the morning here, and it feels so good outside on my balcony."

"Oh, rub it in, will you."

"Couldn't help myself." April laughs. "I'm getting my stuff together. I'll call you back when I get to my rock."

"Okay, later."

Ten minutes later, Chris's phone rings. "I'm here," April says.

"Already?" Chris asks, bewildered. "What, did you run to it?"

"No. My hotel is right next door," She replies, laughing.

"Oh, okay," Chris says. "While we're on the subject of the area, your hotel, is it east or west, or the other two, from the rock? Give me a basic description of the lay of the surrounding area. You know, in case I have to take off running from a herd of elephants or a tiger."

"Let's hope that doesn't happen." April laughs, visualizing one of those two scenarios happening.

Chris says, "I hope it doesn't either. It is much too hot to be running all willy-nilly, but anyway, what's the lay of the land around your rock?"

April answers, "Well, if I'm facing north, I have a parking lot that connects the two hotels on either side of me. The parking lot ends at a four-lane road about fifty yards away. The hotels are about the same distance away on both sides, say thirty yards. I'm walking south now. Not much light this way. I'm on the beach. I haven't been on the beach since I got here. Oh, there's a drop-off. I'm about twenty yards from the rock. I can't tell how far down it is. My flashlight is not very strong. I can hear the waves crashing though."

Chris replies, "Okay, it sounds like you don't have too much room to roam around. I hope the wild animals stay away. When we get connected, I'll have plenty of space so you can walk back to your hotel and get on the elevator to break us apart."

"Sounds good, Chris."

"April, there is literally nothing out here. The last town I remember seeing, I think it was Dkar, was miles and miles ago. I haven't seen anything resembling civilization since Dkar."

"You went through Dkar?" April asks, worry creeping into her voice.

"I did," Chris replies. "The people who saw me just looked at me as I drove by and then went on about their business. But seriously, April, I am feeling uncomfortable out here. Let's get this done quickly so I can get on the road before it gets dark."

"I agree, Chris, and get you home."

"Yeah, that too," Chris grins. "Okay. I am at the red flag on my GPS. I'm going to stop here and get out and look for it. By the way, do you need to pee?"

April answers, "No, I'm good this time. Already taken care of. How about you?"

"Just finished."

"Gross. While you were talking to me?"

"You asked. I wasn't going to say anything until you asked."

"Do you see it?" April asks.

"I see nothing but flat ground and dirt for miles."

"Are you parked on top of it?" she asks.

"Good question," Chris answers. "Are these coordinates you gave me dead on the mark? Let me look under the jeep. Nope. Nothing different under here."

"It has to be there somewhere close by."

"Well, there definitely isn't an arrow overhead pointing down to it."

"Funny." Chuckles April. "Walk around, see if there are any high spots or different colored dirt."

Chris walks in a circle around his jeep widening out each time he passes the front bumper.

"Aye!" exclaims Chris about twenty yards from the front of the jeep.

"What?" asks April.

"Don't you hate it when you're walking and the ground rises, you can't see it and are not expecting it, but it buckles your knees and makes you stumble. That just happened. There is a little rise right here." He marks an "X" in the dirt with his shoe. "I'm going to grab my shovel."

Back at his mark, Chris begins to dig. After ten minutes of digging, drenched of sweat from the heat, Chris says to April, "It's too hot for manual labor. Lordy, mercy, I am soaking wet."

April replies, jokingly, "Just dig. Quit your whining."

"Hmmph." Chris grunts. "This coming from someone whose rock was found for her."

"I know. Shame on me. I should be more sensitive." April laughs, rolling her eyes. "I wish you could see the trencher machine that hit this rock. I'm standing here looking at what is left of it. This rock tore it up."

"Maybe you can send me pictures of it."

Chris stabs his shovel in the dirt again and hears a *bing* from the shovel. He wipes away the dirt from where the shovel hit the rock. The black glassy surface of the rock appears. "Found it," he says into his headset, wiping sweat from his eyes. He continues to clear the area around the whole rock.

Finishing clearing the dirt, Chris is fascinated by the size of this rock. He says to April, "Good grief, this thing is huge."

April remarks, "mine measured thirty-six inches across at its widest point."

"Eyeballing this one, I would say it is about that big too. It definitely is a lot bigger than the one in Argentina."

"I know," April says. "It's amazing."

"It is that," Chris replies, staring down at his rock. "Question, April. Do you think this rock might be more powerful than the

Argentina rock, because it's bigger, or do you think it's probably the same strength?"

"I don't know. We'll have to touch it and see what happens. That's all we can do." April says, excitedly with no hint of worry in her voice.

"Okay. Just a little concern on my part. Shall we touch it and see if it's the same rock?" Chris asks, feeling a little apprehensive.

"I'm ready," April responds, with the same enthusiasm.

"All right, on three. Ready. One, two, three. And hands off. That really tingled. Did yours, April?"

Silence on his headset.

"April? Are you there? April? Talk to me, April!"

More silence.

"Come on, April. Answer me. This isn't funny. April?"

"Chris, hey, this is Tom. April is out. She placed her hand on the rock and started convulsing, like she had been electrocuted, and then went down on the ground. She's not moving."

"Oh no. Tom, can you tell if she is breathing? Is she alive?"

"I don't know. I think I better call 911."

"Hold on, Tom. Hold on before you do that. Let's see if she's breathing first. Can you tell? Is her chest rising up and down?" Chris calms down from panicking. "Can you get down to her nose and see if you can hear her breathe?"

Calming down also, after watching April, Tom replies, "Let me see. She's down beside the rock with her face turned toward the rock. I might have to move her a little."

"No! No!" Chris hollers. "Don't move her. She might be hurt internally. Let's think for a second. Do you have something like a piece of glass or something shiny you can put under her nose?"

"I don't know, Chris. Hang on. Let me look around. Nothing in her equipment bag that I see. Nothing laying on the ground around me. I don't see anything," Tom says, nervously. After a moment of looking around more, Tom hollers out, "Wait! I have a glass in my room. I'll go get it."

"Don't leave her, Tom! Look around everywhere around you. There has got to be something. How about…do you have on a watch?"

"Yes. I do. The watch lens. Hang on, Chris."

A second or two goes by. Chris can hear Tom shuffling around.

"She's breathing!" Tom announces. "The lens fogged up. I'm going to move her out of this hole she is in."

Relieved she is breathing, Chris says, "Okay. Be gentle with her, Tom."

"I will." Chris hears a grunt and groan through the headset. "She won't move." Tom stammers.

"Oh, sorry, Tom. I have to move at the same time she does. Ready and go."

"She's out of the hole."

"Okay. How does she look? Does anything look broken? How is she?"

"As far as I can tell, she looks fine. I think I should call 911 now. In case I'm missing something."

"Tom, as much as I hate to say this, do not call 911."

"But she might need a doctor."

"Tom, I understand the situation, but listen to me. April and I are magnetized together. 911 will send an ambulance. The paramedics will have to move her to the ambulance and on to the hospital. I have to move with her just like a minute ago. Are you following me, Tom? I don't think I can run fast enough to keep up with an ambulance. That puts us in another situation."

"I understand, but what if she is hurt really badly?"

"Tom, I'm very concerned too, very much. Please don't think I'm only thinking of myself and the situation of me having to keep up with a speeding ambulance. I'm not. I'll run until I can't for her. But I think we should wait for her to regain consciousness and, then, see if she wants to go to the hospital. We can break the magnetism, and you can take her."

"Chris, I thought you still loved her?"

"I do, Tom, very much. Think, though. Think about the situation we are in. Are you going to explain to the paramedics our situation?"

A long silence follows.

"Chris, I think you are right. We should wait. It's just… I care very much about her too. That's why I'm here in Hawaii, to be with her."

"So you're the reason she had to be in Hawaii, and I was sent over here. She said she had to talk with some people. I guess you are the people she had to talk with." Chris is getting a sense that he had been used.

"Sorry, man. I tried to get her to tell you about us," Tom lies.

"So tell me, Tom, how long have you two been together?"

"Pretty much since you and her parted ways," Tom lies again.

"Well, I must have missed something, somewhere, huh?" Chris questions, feeling flabbergasted.

"Again, Chris, I'm sorry she didn't say anything to you about us. I'm guessing you're probably not liking hearing this from me. April was supposed to have told you when she first contacted you about Argentina, but I guess she never did." The lies just keep pouring out of Tom.

"No, she never said anything about you two." Chris is hurt and resenting the fact that April misled him into thinking him and her were possibly moving back toward each other. He continues. "So Tom, were you with her when I called to tell her I was close to this rock?"

"I was in the bed next to her when you called," Tom lies again. He is enjoying stirring the pot. He knows April would be upset with him again, but he does not care.

"Huh, she didn't mention you at all the whole time we were talking. She even said she was in a room by herself," Chris says, suspicion entering his mind the more he and Tom talk. "Well, anyway, Tom, call me, or better yet, have April call me when she comes too please. We'll get this magnetism broken, and I can get back to my life, and you two can carry on. And please, don't call 911."

"I will tell her to call you, and I will not call 911. I promise. Later, man." Tom smiles as he puts his phone away. He looks down at April and puts his hand on her forehead and says to her, "It's going to be all right, sweetheart. We are almost free of him."

Chapter 10

Chris sits down on the edge of the hole he had dug around the rock. He is upset, upset from the conversation he had with Tom. He stares at the rock, worrying about April. This rock is a lot bigger than the one in Argentina. He replays in his mind when he touched the rock in La Quiaca and the tingling sensation he felt from it. This rock in front of him has more of a jolt. That jolt is probably more than April could handle, and it knocked her unconsciously.

April is not a very big person. She is a petite woman, who weighs maybe a hundred pounds soaking wet. He kicks at a smaller rock that is on the ground at his feet. He is thinking about April and what that jolt did to her. He is thinking what it must have felt like to her. He hopes she will be all right and will wake up soon. He pictures her laying on her side, as Tom says she was, her eyes closed and that light snore she does when she sleeps. He has to look up, out over the landscape, to get her image out of his head. Sitting here, tearing his heart out over her, is not doing him any good. He looks as far as he can, trying to find something to focus on.

The heat here in the Botswana desert is very intense. Sitting out here, baking in the sun, and sweating profusely, he wishes like anything that he could walk over to the back of the jeep and grab an ice-cold bottle of water from the cooler. He knows that is not possible without April. Realizing if he thinks of something else, he is going to get depressed even more. He decides to try and figure out the April and Tom relationship. As weird as that sounds to him, it irks him that she never mentioned it to him. He leans back and stretches his legs out. He smiles and thinks out loud, *I could've handle it.*

He knew she would find someone else after they fell apart. She is a strong, independent woman, smart, with good looks, and a wonderful personality. But Tom, Tom Henderson, her boss—shaking his head, he thinks, *I'm not understanding. Tom is a player. April told me this the day she introduced me to him. I even kidded her about wanting to go out with him later on in our relationship. She told me, "Not even on a dare would I ever stoope that low," and Tom told me himself that he likes younger women.*

So what changed? Tom said they have been together since April and I parted. "I just don't see it, them two together. Call me crazy, but I really don't," Chris says out loud and then looks around to make sure no one heard him. No one did. He realizes he has not seen anyone in hours, since the drive here. Considering the unbearable heat he is sitting in, he wonders if the hallucinations were about to start.

He finds himself kicking at the rock by his foot again. He does not have any recollection of starting to kick it, but that is what he is doing at the moment. He can feel the heat grow more intense with each passing minute. He knows it will be a futile attempt to try to get to the jeep for some water. Without April's help, he knows he cannot walk to the jeep.

Laying on his back now, he closes his eyes. The glaring sun is not directly above him; it is late afternoon, but it still shines bright even with his eyes closed. He can see dancing floaters bouncing around on his eyelids.

He dozes off for a minute. A shadow passes over him, causing him to jump up. Startled from the sudden awakening, looking around to see if he can find the source of the shadow, his eyes as big as saucers, he cannot find anything in the air around him. *Here we go,* he thinks to himself. *I am starting to see things that is not there. Darn this heat. Darn this rock. Darn April and Tom.*

He lays back and stretches. Images of April enter his mind, April and him laughing at something, something said or something they saw; his mind does not elaborate. He smiles at the image. He sees her clearly. Almost like she is right there with him. He can hear her laugh and hear her talking. He lays there, eyes closed, sweat drying on his skin. He knows he is roasting in the heat. He does not care. April is here with him.

Another image forms in his mind: the night he met April. He knows this story. He plays it over and over a lot, especially when he daydreams while he is driving down the road on a long run.

Tina Gordon set them up on a blind date. Chris was good friends with Tina's husband, and Tina knew April from a gym they went to before April started working with Tina at the college.

Chris was cornered by Tina one day when he was helping Rodney repair his truck. Tina said, "I have a friend whom I want to set you up with. You will like her. She is kind of quiet but has a great personality when she gets comfortable with people. You would be perfect for her."

"How?" I asked.

"Because I know you will," Tina replied.

Tina set up the date. April and I were to meet at a steakhouse, downtown, on a Saturday evening.

I am not the nervous type, at least I did not think I was, but that Saturday, I could not wait for this date. I did not know why. I did not know this girl. All I knew about her is what Tina told me. The anticipation got the better of me, so I went to the restaurant early. I figured I would get to the restaurant and check her out when she came in through the doors. Tina had built her up without any pictures. She told me she is cute, but I should not judge. Just go and have fun.

I arrived and parked my truck. I got out and was walking across the parking lot when I heard my name called. Stepping out of her car was the cutest woman I had ever seen. She approached me and stuck her hand out to me.

"Chris?" she asked in the softest, sweetest voice I had ever heard.

"Yes," I answered, looking into the prettiest hazel eyes. "April?"

"Yes," she said.

We smiled at each other while we checked each other out.

I said, looking back into those hazel eyes, "We're both early. You didn't happen to have the same idea I had, did you?"

"What idea did you have?" she asked.

"I came early to check you out when you came in," I said, smiling sheepishly at her.

She started laughing. "I'm guilty. That is exactly the same idea I had."

We hugged each other.

"Were you going to run if you didn't like what you saw?" she asked, stepping back from our embrace.

"No. I don't play like that. I like to give things a chance."

She smiled.

"What about you?" I asked her.

"I'll play along for a bit. Honestly, I have never been on a blind date, so yes, I'm a little nervous."

"Well, if it makes you feel any better, I'm nervous too. Anyway, how did you know who to look for?"

She said, "Tina described you perfectly, to a 'tee.'"

"Let me guess, all the way to my bald head?"

"Yeah, she did say you were hair-challenged. Tina's words, not mine," she said, looking at my dome. "That doesn't bother me. Should we go in?"

"Yes, ma'am. After you."

We were seated, our drink order taken, and after some more small talk, we placed our food orders and became comfortable with each other.

"So Tina said you own your own business?"

"Yes, I own my own truck and trailer. I'm a truck driver."

April sat back in her seat, and the expression on her face went sour after I told her my profession. I looked at her, proud of myself. I asked her, "Is something wrong?"

She looked over at me for a second with hatred in her eyes. She leaned forward, looked down at the floor, then back at me, returned the smile, and said, "No, I'm sorry. I need to go to the restroom."

She took off to the back of the steakhouse. Our food arrived while she was gone. Five minutes later, she was back.

We were quiet, eating our food. I looked over at her and asked, "Is it okay if I ask what you do when you're not a student?"

"Oh, not much. I go to the gym. That's where Tina and I became friends. She's actually trying to get me a job with the college. I read a lot. I'm kind of boring." The smile and friendliness were back.

"What did you do before you went to school?" I asked.

"I took care of my parents. I started college right out of high school. Mom and Dad were in a wreck one day. The doctors said that Mom suffered severe head trauma. They said my dad would be paralyzed from the neck down." She stopped for a second and took a drink.

"I'm so sorry," I said, looking at her with my heart in my throat.

She looked over the table at me. "It's okay. I can talk about it now. They needed twenty-four-hour care. The insurance company sent a nurse to live with us for a little while, and then, for some reason, the insurance cancelled our coverage. My dad did all he could do to fight the insurance people, but money was really tight while the lawyers were fighting the other party. Dad finally had to ask the nurse to leave. She showed me what to do, and I took care of them until they passed. My mom passed first about a year after the accident. She had taken the brunt of the impact. She really surprised us making it that long. Even the doctors were amazed. My dad took it real hard after she passed. He started having seizures and a couple strokes, but he outlived everyone's predictions. He passed a couple of years ago."

I looked at her and said, "I am so sorry. That had to be absolutely the worst." I took her hands in mine. "Was it another car that hit them, if it's all right for me to ask?"

"No. It was a semitruck that ran a red light." She squeezed my hands as if to say she was okay now.

I lowered my head and looked down at the floor. Now I knew what that look was from earlier.

She patted my hand with hers. "It's okay. I'm okay with it. I told myself in the restroom that it wasn't your fault. And it's not. I can't blame every truck driver."

I looked up at her and shook my head. "You are an amazing woman. I know we just met, but I want you to know that."

"Thank you," she said, clearing her throat. "Anyway, we finally received an enormous settlement from the trucking company. Dad and I lived off that, and after he passed, I continue to use that money. But as goes with most things, it is dwindling down. So you have kids?" She changed the subject, and her parents were never mentioned again by me, out of respect for her.

Chris felt like something was stinging him on the hip. It was not a painful sting, but it kept pulsing. He realized what it was when reality came back to him. It is his phone vibrating and ringing at the same time. He pulls it from its holster and looks at the screen. April's name shows on it. He pushes the green icon on the screen, holds it to his ear, and yawns and says, "Tom," at the same time.

"No, Chris, it's me, "April answers, softly, still feeling the effects of being knocked out.

"April! Oh thank goodness. Are you all right?" Chris smiles and fist-pumps the air.

She answers, "I think so. I am a little sore in places. I've got a nice goose egg on the side of my head. I guess I hit my head on the rock when I went down. I definitely know one thing for sure. This rock has more punch to it than the Hong Kong rock does."

"Yes, it does." Chris agrees, laughing.

"Did you get hurt by it too?" she asks.

"No," he answers. "I guess I have a higher tolerance for pain."

April retorts. "You are bigger than me also."

"Yeah, that, too." Chris chuckles. "You're sure you're all right? You don't need to go to the hospital, do you?"

"I'll be fine," April replies. "I'm tougher than I look."

"Well okay. Is Tom still there?"

"Yes, he's here."

"Good," Chris says and then asks, "by the way, how come you didn't say anything about you two?"

"What? Us two?" April is surprised by this revelation. She turns and glares at Tom.

"Yeah, he said you two have been seeing each other for a while. You could have told me."

"Oh, really. He did, did he?" April stares at Tom, who begins squirming around, trying to avoid her. She is fuming mad. "Let's talk about this some other time. Right now, we need to concentrate on getting ourselves demagnetized."

"Actually, I need to get to my water first. I am definitely cooking out here, probably real close to a heat stroke."

"Yes. Which way do you need to go?"

"Um, north."

"How far, Chris? I can't go south too far, you know that."

"It's just under twenty yards to the jeep."

"I sure hope so." April worries. "Go when you're ready."

"Here I go," Chris says.

"Chris, stop!" April exclaims. "That's as far as I can go. I'm at the ledge."

"Oh no. I'm at the front bumper of the jeep. The water is in the back. Can you go another ten feet?"

"No, I can't go anymore. I am on the edge. One more step and I go down. Chris, I'm so sorry."

"Jeez, I am so thirsty."

"Okay, let me think." Chris looks over the jeep and around it for anything that might work. There is nothing around. An idea occurs to him. "April, here is what I'm going to do. I'm going to open the hood on the jeep, take my belt buckle, and touch it to the positive battery terminal. See if that will break our magnetism."

"You are not going to electrocute yourself!" April shouts. "Chris, no!"

"What other choice do I have?"

"I can go to the hotel, and we can do the elevators magnetic field again," April pleads.

"I don't think I can make it. I am literally about to pass out. Listen, I will call you back as soon as I'm done. Okay?"

"You better, and you better not get yourself dead."

"I promise I will not die, April. Bye for now."

"Bye, Chris. I lo—" Her phone beeps, telling her he has disconnected. She almost starts crying.

Chapter 11

April turns toward Tom, who has followed her to the ledge. She stares at him with an intensity that could burn a hole through him. She is so mad at him for telling Chris that him and her are dating and have been for a while.

"How dare you, Professor Henderson." April hisses, wide-eyed. "We are not dating, and we are certainly not serious. We go out, sometimes. Ugh. Why would you do such a thing? Chris has been nothing but kind and wonderful helping with this project. He is even using his own money for this. I have realized what a big mistake I made. Chris and I were working great together. I have hope for us. But now, thanks to you. How could you? How could you be so shallow? Huh?"

Tom looks down at the ground. He actually feels bad for his actions.

"You are something else," April continues. "Since you have ruined any hope I have with Chris, at least tell me that he will be reimbursed for his expenses."

Tom looks at April, shuffled his feet, kicked at a rock, and finally shook his head "no."

"No, what? No, you're not going to tell me?" April asks, still fuming.

Tom keep his eyes turned toward the ground. He swallows hard and says, "They are not going to reimburse him. They said he volunteered for this. Therefore—"

"He did not volunteer!" April shouts, cutting Tom off. "I asked him if he would. You said to ask him. Did you tell them that?"

"I did," Tom says, giving April his "I'm-sorry" look. "They said they officially documented him as a volunteer to the project. They said they don't compensate volunteers. That's a strict policy that can't be changed. They aren't going to give him any mention of being involved in these discoveries either."

Tears streams down April's cheeks. She cannot believe what she heard Tom just say. "Are you serious? Oh my God. He has spent nearly ten thousand dollars of his own money. He has done everything I needed him to do. You're telling me that the people in charge of this are not going to give him one iota of credit for his part or repay him his money. Who the hell do these people think they are? Let me talk to them. This is not going to happen this way."

Tom shuffles his feet some more. He looks at April. He looks over the edge into the darkness below. He looks back at April and says, "Dear, I'm sorry. I told them we were using several volunteers with this, not just Chris. The budget they gave me for this project covered enough for you and only you. I had to twist some arms to get more money for me to join you on this. After the discovery you and Chris made on the Hong Kong/Argentina rock, I got selfish. I wanted to share the glory with you. I'm deeply and madly in love with you, so I moved Chris out of the picture. They don't know he's in Africa. As far as they know, he volunteered for Argentina and went home afterward."

April takes one step away from the ledge and one step toward Tom. She slaps him hard, across the face. She cannot speak. Words are forming in her head, but her mouth is not moving. She spits in Tom's face and turns and storms off toward the hotel.

April hears Tom say behind her, "Chris's trick must have worked. You're moving freely."

April raises her left hand into the air with her middle finger standing alone and kept walking.

April enters her hotel room and goes to a chair by the window. She pulls out her phone from her back pocket and pushes the phone icon on the screen. Chris's name is at the top of the list. She pushes his name to call him.

Chris answers his headset on the second ring. "Hey, girl." He says sounding hoarse. "You still okay?"

April gasps when she heard Chris's voice and how hoarse he sounded. She asks, "Are you all right? You sound horrible."

"I'm fine. I've been sitting here on the back of my jeep drinking water and pouring water over my head. I almost overheated myself. As for the shock, I took from the battery, I don't think I have any permanent damage. But let me tell you, that was a hit I was not expecting. That was a big, big ouch."

Laughing at Chris and his silliness, April says, "I couldn't wait any longer for you to call me. I was too scared something bad might have happened to you. Thank goodness you're all right, physically."

"Are you taking shots at my mentality, April? Anyway, have we proven that this rock and your rock are the same?"

"Yes, we have," April answers.

"Does this mean we are done?"

Crying now, April says, "Yes. We are done. You can come home, Chris." She does not want to cry. She knows he can hear her, but she is overcome with emotion. She wants to keep him on the phone until he returns home, but she knows that is not possible. She fears this might be the end for her and him. With what Tom has told him and Tom being here with her now, how could she convince him she and Tom are not together? And of course, the revelation that he is not going to be reimbursed anything or have any recognition for the discoveries.

Hearing her crying, Chris asks, "Are you crying because we are finished, or are these happy tears or something else?"

"It's something else mainly. I'll have to tell you about it later. I can't do it right now."

"Let me guess. Tom did something stupid?"

April answers, "He did, but that's not all. Just come home, please. We'll talk then, face to face."

"Well, I know not to press you when your upset, so do you have all the information you need? No more rocks to go find?"

"Yes, I have all the information, and no…no more rocks to find that I know of."

Losing some of the hoarseness in his voice, Chris says, "All righty, I'll start making my way home. And April, whatever Tom did that was stupid, just slap him one good one."

"I already did," she says with a chuckle. "You be careful and call me when you get home."

"I will. Bye, April."

"Bye, Chris." She wanted to say "love you," but she held it back.

The phone goes silent. April sits in her chair, staring out her room's window, tears coming heavily from her eyes. She knows she has to figure out some way to repay Chris and his expenses. She sits and ponders what to do. Nothing came to her. She will have to find something. The last thing she wants is Chris mad at her and thinking she lied and used him.

She stares out the window for the rest of the night.

Chapter 12

Chris stares at the rock for what seems like forever before loading up his stuff in the jeep. The reality of what they have discovered finally hit him. The world is held together by rocks that go all the way through to the other side. Like a rebar that they use to hold concrete together, these rocks are following that principle. Sliding into the driver's seat, he takes one last look at the rock. "How many more are there?" he asks out loud. He cranks the engine and starts the journey back to Johannesburg.

As he starts to put miles behind him, he thinks about April. They have gotten along great with each other the past few weeks. It is kind of like him and her never stopped their relationship. They had a pause and picked right back up where they left off, though this whole time has been on the phone. Maybe when he gets back home, she will see him. He smiles at that thought.

He drives on seeing her in his mind, her smile and her laugh, the way he remembers her as being a simple, low-maintenance girl. He smiles some more.

The thought of the past few weeks enters his mind, and Tom Henderson. Tom was out with them the night before he was told he was too immature, as was Tina and her husband. Everything seemed fine between April and him. Was that when they decided they liked each other? Tom is more immature than he is. He stares at the road.

He shakes the negative thoughts out of his head. *Tom and April are together. There's no need for me to be in their way. If I can remain friends with April, then a friend I will be.*

He thinks about that scenario for a bit. *I will have to be friendly with both of them if these discoveries blow up like I guess they will. We changed history. We changed the way the people of the world will look at planet Earth now. It is held together by rock rebars. I think I can maintain a friendliness with them two through all the publicity that we will be going through. And they owe me a lot of money.*

Arriving in Johannesburg, Chris drives straight to the airport. Along the way, he makes the decision to be a man and accept the fact that April has Tom. He will play his part and be happy.

Sitting in the lounge at the airport waiting on his flight home to be announced, Chris sees April and Tom appear on the television, with "breaking news" scrolling across the bottom of the screen. He moves closure to the television so he can hear.

"Mr. Henderson?" a reporter starts.

"Dr. Henderson please." Tom smiles at the reporter.

"Sorry. Dr. Henderson, you and Mrs. Mckenzie are claiming to have discovered rock formations that appear to be holding the Earth together, is that correct?" the reporter asks.

Tom looks at the reporter and flashes a smile, while April stands by his side with a sour look on her face. "Yes, that is correct."

"And where are these rock formations located?" the same reporter asks.

Tom answers with the same beaming smile. "We found one here in Honolulu, and the other one we found in Hong Kong."

"You said earlier they go through the Earth to the other side, correct?" asks another reporter.

Tom answers, "Yes, they do. The one here in Honolulu goes through to Botswana, in Africa, and the one in Hong Kong goes through to Argentina."

"Are these the only two? Are there any more?" asks the same reporter.

Still smiling, Tom replies, "Well, there are other researchers out looking for others, but these two have been confirmed by myself and Mrs. Mckenzie and other people."

"Who are the other people?"

April starts to answer, but Tom cuts her off. "Scientists and archeologists."

Chris stares at the television astounded. There is no mention of him being involved in the discoveries. Tom and April are going to take all the credit for themselves.

Chris returns to his seat, ignoring the rest of the press conference. He sits and stares at the floor. After a few minutes, he reaches the conclusion that that must have been the reason that April was crying earlier. Tom told her not to mention me or acknowledge that I was a part of this. He wants him and her to have all the glory.

They can have it, Chris says to himself, looking out the window of the airport lounge. *Just pay me back my money for my part. That is all I want anyway. You two can have all the fame and glory. Give me my money back, and I will wish you two the best of luck.*

Chris stews about the situation. He tries telling himself to let it be, but he cannot. He grabs his phone and pushes April's name on the screen.

April answers her phone, "Hey, Chris. Where are you?"

"I'm in Johannesburg waiting on my flight. I just saw Tom and you on the television and thought I would call and congratulate you two on your discoveries. You two must be on cloud nine." Chris is being very sarcastic. "Is that the game you two are playing? You two made the discoveries and nobody else? Really!"

April can hear the anger in Chris's voice. "Chris, I'm sorry." April is trying not to get upset. "Yes, Tom is telling everyone that he and I made these discoveries."

Chris hollers at her. "And you're going along with his scheme?" Other people in the lounge turned to look at Chris. "April, come on."

"I have no choice, Chris. My name and his name are on all the research. I have to."

"You have to, my ass, April. Is he there with you, now? Let me talk to him."

"He's not here. I'm in my room packing to go home. I don't know where he is, and *I don't care.*"

"I'm not going to be reimbursed my money, am I?" Chris asks calmly, after hearing April yell.

April cannot hold it any longer. She starts crying. "No, not by the ones who funded this project. I am so sorry. Chris, I will try and pay you back somehow myself. I promise."

"Don't bother. You two have a happy life together. You two so deserve each other. And April, you called me the immature one."

Chris ends the call.

April cries.

Chris arrives at his house quietly. After showering, unpacking, and starting his laundry, he kicks back in his recliner. He turns on the television. Flipping through the channels, he happens upon a show featuring Tom and April's discovery. A picture of the two of them came on, showing them looking happy together. He turns off the television.

Chris leans back in his recliner and closes his eyes. He reopens them thirty minutes later when he hears a knock at his front door. He gets up and goes to open the door. Two men in white button downs, black ties, and black pants are standing on the porch.

"Are you Chris Collier?" one of the white button downs asks.

"I am. And you are?" Chris asks, looking them both up and down.

"We're with the US Government. We need to have a word with you."

"Am I in trouble for something?" Chris asks.

"No, sir," replies the button down on the right.

"Do you guys have identification?"

They show their identification. "May we speak with you?"

"Yes," Chris says. "Come in. Would you guys like something to drink?"

"No, thanks," says one of the button downs. "Let us get straight to the point of why we're here. April Mckenzie told about your part in the two rock discoveries and how much you spent of your own money. We are here to make a proposal to you to get your money back plus a whole lot more."

"Okay, I'm listening." Chris smiles.

"You are a truck driver, correct?"

"Yes, I am." Chris answers.

"Okay. So our proposal to you is this. The US government would like for you to go to Afghanistan and haul military equipment from place to place. We will put you under contract as an independent contractor for six months. We will pay you two hundred thousand US dollars for those six months. After your six months, you may return home and go back to your regular routine, or come home for a month and go back for another six months under a new contract."

"You guys planning on being there that long?" Chris asks seriously.

Ignoring Chris's question, one of the white button downs asks, "So what do you say?"

"When do you need to know by? I haven't been home long. I haven't seen my parents or kids yet. I'll need to talk it over with them anyway."

"We understand, Mr. Collier. Can you let us know by this time next week?"

"That I can do."

"Here's our contact information. Let us know either way."

"I will. Thanks, guys."

"You should probably thank Ms. Mckenzie. She was adamant about repaying you when we talked to her by herself.

Chris shakes their hands and shows them out. He sits back in his recliner and thinks. He thinks of what April had said to him, how she would pay him back his money somehow. She promised. Looks like she found a way. Chris smiles. "She knows I love an adventure."

The End

About the Author

Christopher Gardner lives in Oneonta, Alabama, with his wife, Angie. They have four kids and three grandkids. This is Christopher's first book. In his free time, when Christopher is not working or writing, he and Angie like to get out and find antiques.